HE WHO DOES NOT EXIST

VICTORIA W THOMSON

HE WHO DOES NOT EXIST

First edition. July 25, 2025.

ISBN: 979-8998841613

Written by Victoria W Thomson.

Table of Contents

Dedications

To my husband, Brian: I love you. Thank you for everything. I thank God for you everyday.

To my daughter, Alison: I love you. Please read a book, any book. You are My Sunshine. My only sunshine.

To Robin: Thank you so much for being the beta reader. In fact, I think you might be an alpha reader. You had to read it, while it was still being written.

THE BOOKFEST®
AWARDS

Fall 2025

He Who Does Not Exist

Victoria W Thomson

Third Place

Christian – Fantasy

THE BOOKFEST
This award acknowledges your
contribution to the world
of literature and books.

Thank you and congratulations,

Desiree Duffy
Desiree Duffy
Founder

Revelation 13:18 states, "This calls for wisdom: let the one who has understanding calculate the number of the beast, for it is the number of a man, and his number is 666".

Chapter 1 First Class

Penny is excited to be in the competition for Hell's elite position of lead soul catcher. If selected, she will no longer have to get her hands dirty, actually catching the souls. *Good*, she thinks, *I'm tired of that and I have already mastered it, if I do say so myself.*

If selected, she will be in management. She loves the idea of being in charge, and of having subordinate demons. If selected, she will be in charge of the ones, who actually get the souls. There are a lot of ifs, but Penny is ready and excited. This means she'll be on Earth temporarily and mortal temporarily. She will not have her demon powers. She will still have her intelligence and her compulsion to succeed and be better than everyone else. She checked on that.

Now on Earth and mortal, she sticks her head into the classroom door and looks at the other students. She sees the other seven demons in the class and sizes up her competition. She knows the other demons well and she is not concerned. She can explain her sin and how her sin, pride, gets people into Hell, better than anyone else. She confidently takes her seat in the front of the room.

The teacher walks in from the top doors of the lecture hall down to the podium. Everyone turns staring. They can't believe it's him. He's wearing a dark pinstriped suit. As he makes his way to the bottom of the stairs, he turns, and faces the class.

"So you are my class of honor students, honor demons, as it were. I am the devil. Boo!" The class is staring transfixed on every word he is saying. They were too in awe to react when he said boo.

"I know you were expecting something different, but here is the big thing: we need to move in the shadows. We can't be flashy. We can't let everyone know it's us. Sometimes that works in our favor, but, usually, it doesn't. Usually, you need to work quietly in the background and have no one know you are or were there.

"So let me explain, how this class is going to work because you are supposed to be the best of my demons. You are the ones who are going to be in charge of the new demons, who harvest souls. It will be your job to train the newly promoted demons on how to get souls. As in, they will be helping people - go to Hell! Well, to be honest, the people were probably already going to go to Hell. Your trainees just make it so it's a little more likely.

"Also while all of you are elite demons and will be in charge of other underling demons, one of you will be selected as the lead soul catcher. The lead soul catcher works directly with me and will be in charge of the all the departments.

"So here is how this class is going to work. I will have each of you describe the infamous deadly sin that you represent and how it gets people into Hell. I figured this was as good a place to start as any," says the devil.

With that he moves into the thoughts of one of the students, Penny, who is sitting there quietly taking notes, very studiously.

He gets into her thoughts and says, *Hi. Yes, I am quite capable of being in your thoughts and as you will soon learn, you can do it too. Now, here is the best part, no one knows when we're here. When you are here, inside someone's mind, not only will you be able to read the mortal's thoughts, you can kind of influence them. I've chosen you, Penny, because you were having quite a few thoughts while taking your notes. You seem very serious, so I figured it was only fair for me to make a personal appearance.*

Penny opens her eyes real wide and looks at the devil. She looks at his whole body rather than making direct eye contact. The devil notices this and makes direct eye contact with Penny, who then immediately looks him in his eyes.

The devil then says, "That's better." The devil now addresses the class.

"Well class, I'm going to go grab one of the mortals from Earth. The mortal will just think he is having a bad dream or something. I'm going to get inside his mind. I want you to all start bringing yourself into his mind.

"This is different from how you have previously viewed the mind of the mortal. Previously, you were assigned a mortal and told what to do. Now, you will learn to pick any mortal and determine which sin will work best at damning that mortal.

"Here is the hierarchy. Obviously, I am at the top. Next down is the lead soul catcher. This is the demon who can look at any mortal and determine what sin is going to damn them. Once the lead soul catcher knows which sin is to be used, the appropriate department will be contacted. As department heads, you will in turn, send in one of the underling demons. So to sum up, by being in this class you are already department heads. Congratulations. We are here to see which one of you will be the lead soul catcher. There is only one.

The class looks at each other and smiles. This is the first time they have been told they are department heads. Most of them hope to be more.

"Back to getting into a mortal's head. You just look at them. You think about them and then you think what does this person want most. What is going to do it for them. What is the thing that is going to let you in. What is their weakness? Don't worry, while you are in this class, I can help you have full demon powers, but only while you are in this class."

Suddenly, next to him appears a very disheveled person, kind of scared, kind of terrified actually and he looks up at the students, not knowing the students are actually newly mortal demons.

The devil says, "Tell me, why are you here?"

The person responds, "I don't know man. I-I dropped some acid and I guess I'm on a bad trip."

The devil looks at the class.

"Well class, this is as good a place to start as any. Let's do some roll call and have one of you get into this person's head.

"Lust, my darling, my vixen, why don't you start."

She looks at the person, suddenly she can see or rather just knows all the mortal thoughts, and then says, "Oh, what is it you want most? Let's see, oh you'll do fine, by which I mean, I'll do fine. You find women attractive, not in any way that you want a relationship, but you do certainly want to sleep with some of them. So let's see what we can make happen. Oh, I can feel all his thoughts, oh this will be fun."

The devil then says, "All right let's move on to the next mortal." The devil exchanges the disheveled man for one in a suit. The man in the suit looks around confused, his brow furrowed.

"Avarice, you represent cocaine levels of greed. What do you think? Come now, you must have something."

Avarice flashes a knowing smile. He already knows how to do this. "Oh, I can see that he wants more. I can appreciate wanting more. He wants more money, more respect, and more power. He wants more of everything. He just wants more and he doesn't care what he has to do to get it. Oh what else can we do with you, sir? Because I'm pretty sure he's going to do anything to get more." The demon, Avarice, can feel more of what this person is needing, wanting, and coveting.

Then, the devil says, "All right that's enough." With a snap of his fingers, the man in the suit goes away in a puff of smoke.

The devil brings in another mortal. As he does, the door to the classroom opens. The door, before it opens even an inch, causes the devil to make the mortal he just brought in vanish. Everything and everyone looks like a regular college class.

A girl pokes her head in the door, without opening it all the way. "Oh, I didn't realize you were in here, already."

The devil looks at the girl very angrily and snaps, "Yes, I'm here. This class is closed. You shouldn't be here."

The girl smiles, looks directly at all of the students, and closes the door. Penny notices, the devil stares at the door a little too long, like he knew the girl.

HE WHO DOES NOT EXIST

The devil then brings back the mortal, who was there before the girl opened the door. The devil addresses the class as if nothing had happened. "Well Gluttony, what do you think?"

Gluttony knows what the mortal is thinking but it's fuzzy. "The guy does seem kind of hungry, but it's more of he wants things prepared in a certain way. Everything done in a certain way. It's more of, he wants all the food, but he wants it prepared very precisely according to his standards.

"All he cares about is indulging, for the sake of indulging, not because he is looking at his fellow man or anything."

Gluttony can't think of anything else to say. He just stops talking and looks down.

The devil says, "Alright, I'm not as happy with that one, but it'll do". Then he looks at Envy, and says, "Envy, what do you think?"

She is careful about answering. It is not enough for her to look good, she must also have the others look bad. Gluttony just did that. She wants to and needs to impress the devil, but doesn't want the other demons to know she is talented. If they under estimate her, they may be less competitive, then she can win more easily.

Envy, who understands with crystal clarity what this person's thinking, answers, "Well, he does want all the riches. He looks at people and wishes he had their power, their cars, their jewels, and their nice house." She looks down.

"I am afraid, I'm just not very good at this. I am just not feeling it as well as the others did.

"He doesn't seem to be envious. He does seem to have a lot of greed. I guess I do feel that he wants more, but I'm not feeling everything."

"Alright, thank you, Envy." The devil thinks to himself 'oh Envy, leaving us wanting more, as always. Of course, that is part of your sin.'

"Sloth, will you try now?"

"What's the point? I mean honestly, I don't care. What's the big deal with us being able to go into someone's mind and read their thoughts and maybe influence them. Why should I waste my time reading a mortal's mind?"

At this point, the devil enlarges himself and no longer appears his suave and sophisticated self. He is huge, he is scary, and he lunges toward Sloth. He looks like a snarling dragon.

"Well the big deal is you want to know what sins they have committed, what sins they want to commit, and what sins they are unlikely to commit.

"The whole big thing is YOU are trying to remove the mortal from "him" (the devil points up). It's like we just need to get rid of any evidence of Christ. If they believe, at all, in Christ, and in the Holy Spirit, and all that; we're not going to get him and we want him. So if we can go into the mortal's mind, and we can and we do then YOU will waste your time on this!

"Oh and Sloth, you will waste your time because it is your job to get his soul. It is why you are in this class, so that is why it is worth your time. Do you understand me? YOU WILL GET THAT SOUL."

The devil returns to his normal size and charming demeanor.

Envy leans over to Penny and says, "At least, I did better than he did." Penny nods.

"Now as I was saying," the devil continues.

"Hey, don't I get a chance? Where's my mortal?" Wrath stands up and asks.

"Fine. I'll bring in a mortal for you," says the devil, rather annoyed that he was interrupted.

A man appears, whose fists are clenched, he is wearing a sweatshirt, and jeans. His hair is dripping with sweat and he looks like he either was in or was about to be in a fight. The man looks around a little confused, which causes him to clench his fists more.

"This one's easy. Obviously, he's filled with anger and rage. He just wants to hit something. He's not looking at the why. It's about the immediate reaction and not even considering any long-term consequences. He is filled with anger and there is no reason." Wrath finishes his assessment of the mortal, having seen everything clearly, and sits down.

"All right, very good. Now, if I can get back to what I was saying?" the devil says, still annoyed at being interrupted.

Wrath doesn't feel he received the sense of acknowledgement from the devil or the others that he feels he deserves. He sits stewing in his anger at the perceived slight.

The devil continues, "Thought implantations, the lovely thing is we just have to plant seeds of doubt. As we plant our seeds of doubt, oh don't they grow deliciously fast and easy. For example watch with just a little bit of planting, I can make this person question their shoes."

With that, he enters the mind of a mortal, picked out at random on Earth, who immediately looks down at his shoes and kind of moves his feet a little bit. Sometimes moving one foot behind the other. The demons can tell he's just, he's just not comfortable with his shoes. Not like oh I'm in pain. More a feeling of 'I'll never make it.' The demons can just tell this mortal is preoccupied with their shoes. The mortal feels like these shoes are not correct for where they are." The demons can sense that's where the mortal's mind is.

The devil stops his example and says, "That's it folks. You do a very small thought implant. You let the seed grow, a little bit, not too much and then, you wait and see. Later, you come back. Basically, you just want the person to worry about anything other than other people's well-being. It's okay for the mortal to worry about other people, like Envy worries about what other people think of her, that's not a problem.

"What we want to do is make the person self-conscious, that they're not good enough, or you want to make them worry about themselves. If they're worried about themselves; they're not worried about their fellow man.

"Here's the big thing with the deadly sins, what makes them deadly is that it separates the mortal from Christ and that's what we need to do. As we explore each deadly sin, you'll see how each sin separates the mortal from Christ. We need to have it so these people turn away from Christ.

"This is where it's even more perfect. Don't forget, we don't exist. There are records from the 1500's saying I convinced the world I don't exist. They keep commenting that it's a trick I played on them. It is known. Yet, they keep falling for it.

"Nowadays science is my best friend. Everyone (by which I mean the mortals) thinks themselves so smart."

The devil stops and looks around the room before settling on Penny, who represents the sin of pride. "Penny you must know this one, quite right up pride's alley." Penny nods, but only half-heartedly.

HE WHO DOES NOT EXIST

The devil continues, "The mortals think they're very smart because they're coming up with all these ways of proving things and studying things. They have just about proven, that if they believe in anything remotely, related to religion then, they're just being silly and provincial. Science is now the truth. They don't look at it like science is letting them learn more about God's world. They make it science or God.

"Well that's fine by me. Science can appear in charge. In fact, thanks to science, I've gotten it so if you believe in God, you're kind of a ninny. Why would you believe in that? It's what, the big invisible guy in the cloud, that's not what you're going to believe in, is it? How about we believe in cellular division, and what goes on with diseases, and how long the Earth's been around.

"I will tell you what it means. I've managed to convince the silly mortals, that by giving up religion, that it is wrong to have a day of rest. I mean to get rid of the Sunday, day of rest. No longer do you get a day of the week off to just rest, breathe, and contemplate how things are going in the world.

"Now, it is always everyday, all day, same grindstone just work, work, work. I used to let you have a whole day off. Well I didn't, God did. He gave them that and I took it away." The devil chuckles at his success.

"Those idiot mortals were like 'no we're progressive, we don't want to be told which day we have off.' My favorite one is, 'it's just wrong to take Sunday, what about Friday, for the Jewish people, or what about Saturday, for the Seventh-Day Adventists.'

"They divided themselves. I love when people divide. I love division. Divide and conquer. They have no idea how easy it is to conquer the divided. So first it started with we will let you have the stores open from 12:00 to 6:00 on Sunday, just a half day. Let some businesses open. Grocery stores, no one is going to die if I can buy a box of graham crackers on a Sunday. Certainly, you wouldn't let someone sell liquor or anything like that. Just a bit of 'okay you can sell some basic necessary supplies on Sunday.' Then, I got it so they can be open all the time. It was no restrictions on hours because we were not going to be following religion.

"I got the people to argue the first amendment right to freedom of religion meant they didn't have to observe Sunday. Silly mortals, it's not that you have to observe Sunday; it's that you get to observe Sunday, a day of rest.

"This gets so much better. I didn't even have to do anything, after a while, people's greed wanted more and more. So, it went from not open at all; to open for a few hours, but people got time and a half. They were paid extra. Well, I just simply had them pass another law. They lost time and a half, and a day of rest. So now, Sunday is a day like any other. It used to be a nice day of rest. They'd see their family. They'd have some Sunday dinner. Ha-ha! Now that everybody's working, there's just not time for Sunday dinner. There is no time for family. There's just not time for a moment of reflection.

"Oh and ever since there's been no religion, there's no time. Everybody started earning more money, but having less. No one goes to church, though, no time. As it's going on now, my next greatest trick might be convincing the world (as he points up) that God doesn't exist. I'm getting closer. You should see the mess the world's in now, but as long as I can keep things going the way they're going; there's no end to what I can accomplish.

"Now, there's a reason we're all sitting here in mortal form. If we were to walk around in all the scary things that they think we are, they would know to put themselves on guard. Let's face it, if a big dragon showed up and said follow me, they'd crap their pants and run to the nearest church. I understand that, so we're not going to do that. No no no. I'm going to be in the sheep's clothing; because that's what's best for me.

"There are still places I cannot manage to go without raising a stink. Even though, 'Hi, I look like everybody else.' Everyone is on such high alert for me, like Salem, Massachusetts during Halloween. Oh my word, those people are crazy. Transylvania is also not going to work. Everyone is on their guard. No, we work best when no one suspects a thing, until it's too late.

"All right, tomorrow, we start on our deadly sins and Lust you get to start us off."

Lust smiles and says, "Oh good, I'll be the virgin speaker."

GREETINGS READER, I'M glad I caught you before the chapter ended. I will be speaking to you throughout the book. It only makes sense. I mean you know, I, the devil, exist. Why shouldn't I know that you, the reader, exist. I mean, let's face it, I'm in a book. Did you not think I wouldn't know where I am and thus, where you are?

Chapter 2 After Class

The demons leave the class. Most of them walk towards the cafeteria. They have a lot to talk about, like just seeing the devil.

Lust is hanging on Wrath's arm, like an accessory. They walk up to the counter. The last of the group to order is Gluttony. The person behind Gluttony is on the phone. Gluttony overhears the person behind him say, "I'm just going to pick up a small cup of coffee and then I will be out to meet you guys. Five minutes tops."

Gluttony chuckles and looks at him out of the corner of his eye. Gluttony places the most complicated order anyone has ever placed for what amounts to a cup of coffee. The poor cafeteria worker is left to try and explain, this is not a coffee house. Gluttony yells at the worker calling him incompetent. Needless to say, it causes problems, a lot of problems. Gluttony doesn't care. He, eventually, gets what can only be described as a big cup of coffee and a frightened, near crying, counter worker. The guy behind him just rolls his eyes and asks for a small cup of black coffee.

Gluttony walks towards the group, who were already seated. Lust and Avarice are talking about what they want from the class.

Lust very explicitly says, "I want that job as lead soul catcher. And I intend to get it, by whatever means necessary." She gives a coquettish smile.

"So you're just going to sleep with the devil to get that job. You think that's gonna work?" Avarice asks, incredulously.

Lust looks at him and says, "Oh honey, I've already been sealing that deal, for a while. I know it's gonna work. I know how good I am."

Avarice looks at her and says, "I'm going to impress him with my skills and my plans. You should hear the plans I have and how many souls I can bring in. When the devil hears how my ideas will bring us people in droves, that job of lead soul catcher is as good as mine. Once the mortals let their greed take over, desperation will come quick. Those mortals will do anything to get out of the problems, their greed has created for them. So, I am not too worried. I am going to get that lead soul catcher job."

"What's your big plan?" Sloth asks.

"You, and everyone else, will have to wait until my presentation." Avarice answers.

Sloth shrugs and says, "I didn't care that much anyway."

Penny finally comes in and joins the group. The group gives her a bit of a look. She says, "Just talking with the devil, seeing if there was anything I should concentrate on while here on Earth to prepare as future lead soul catcher."

Wrath looks at her and says, "Typical Penny, you just assume you will be selected. Everybody knows Penny is the favorite. Why do you go by Penny? The rest of us just use the name of the sin we represent. What do you think makes you so special?"

Penny meets Wrath's intimidating stare, full on, with no hesitation and says, "Well, I worked my freaking butt off to get here. I did everything by myself to get where I am today. I studied hard. I beat out a lot of little underling demons, who wanted to represent pride, to get to this position and I'm going to make damn sure they remember my name. I want them to know who they're answering to and just who is in charge. They are going to know they are answering to Penny. That it was all me, nobody else. I did everything and I want them to know it was me. Don't you want them to know your name?"

Lust then leans in and says "I like to think I just slept my way to the top."

Avarice joins with "I wanted it. I did what I had to do to get it. That's what avarice does. And I represent unrestrained greed. Oh and to answer your little name question. I prefer they refer to me as the embodiment of what I am, avarice."

Lust looks at Envy and asks, "What are you going to do?"

Envy looks at the group and says, "Well, I certainly will not be sleeping with the devil to get what I want; nor will I be coming up with any grand plan like Avarice; nor am I going to beg the devil for extra credit work to become lead soul catcher. Instead, I'm going to ensure the rest of you fail. I don't need to be better than the rest of you, I just need the rest of you to be worse than me. I have no problem being chosen as lead soul catcher by default." The other demons stare at Envy and to a certain degree are impressed by her level of evil.

Despair doesn't say anything. She just sort of sits in the corner, looks down, and wonders, *I don't know how I got here or why. I guess maybe there was a mistake. I definitely don't deserve it.*

Sloth looks up. He sits in his chair, in a very reclined, almost horizontal position. He says, "I can assure you. I did not put in any extra effort to get where I am today. I cut every corner that I could. I am lazy. I don't care about anything or anyone, but I guess that does make me perfect for representing sloth. Not that the devil understood or liked me too much, today."

Wrath says, "No, you ticked him off good. I hope you didn't ruin things for the rest of the class. You should think about others, namely me."

"Relax, I doubt anyone made any long term impressions. It was the first lecture," Sloth adds.

Penny sees a girl. She looks like the girl who interrupted the class. The girl makes direct eye contact with Penny, rolls her eyes at the other demons, and shakes her head.

Penny looks back at the girl quizzically and wonders *who are you'* Penny feels a little uneasy. She turns to the other demons. When Penny looks back less than a minute later, the girl was gone.

Penny then looks at Gluttony and says, "Did you see her?"

He looks at Penny and says, "See who? I can see Lust. I can see Envy. I can see you. What or who am I supposed to see?"

No one sees me, thinks Despair.

Penny explains, "There was a girl sitting over there, a minute ago. I thought it was the girl, who interrupted the class. She gave me a look like I should know who she is."

Penny looks at Sloth and says, "Did you see her? Do you know if it is the girl who interrupted the class?"

"I don't care. I know who I need to know and I don't really want to know them, but, no, I don't see a girl over there. Maybe you're just seeing things."

Penny, feeling kind of tired, says, "Ok, well there's clearly no one there now. I guess, I have gone a little insane."

With that, the group switches topics and Avarice says, "So what did you guys think of seeing the devil? Was he everything we thought he'd be? I mean it was pretty cool when he enlarged himself, while he was yelling at Sloth, which was awesome, in and of itself."

Envy looks at everyone and says, "Yeah, that was pretty awesome when he made himself big like that and yelled at Sloth. I was glad I wasn't Sloth."

Lust adds, "He commanded the room from the moment he walked in. There was no forgetting him and I've been seeing him for quite a while. This is not his first appearance, at least for me."

Avarice glares at Lust rather angrily and says, "Well I'm going to get the job of lead soul catcher, without having to sleep with him, and he's still going to be far more impressed with me than he is with you."

Wrath looks at everyone and says, "I just hope the class didn't get off on the wrong foot with him. I have plans. I need to make sure that I am taken seriously."

Penny says, "Well guys, I've gotta get a tighter grip on all of your sins. Frankly, I know each of you individually is going to make a presentation, but I don't like to rely on other people. So I'm gonna head to my dorm room and make sure, if one of you doesn't give a good presentation, that I still know your sin. We need to know what sin to call in for a particular case. I need to know the content, whether or not you present it well."

Everyone gives Penny a dirty look. She didn't care. With that, she leaves the cafeteria.

No sooner had she gotten to the hallway, then the devil appears right in front of her. She is a little taken aback. He seemed to appear out of nowhere.

"Penny, how are you? Everything going well? Are we adjusting well? You seem a little shaken," he asks, like he didn't already know.

Penny answers, "There was a weird girl in the cafeteria. I almost thought she was the girl who interrupted class. It's a little odd. I'm a little shaken by it. I am sure it is nothing."

The devil looks at her and says in a pacifying voice, "Well, I don't know who you saw because I wasn't there. I wouldn't give her a second thought. Could be someone from the masquerading class at Schomolance Academy, in Hell. They sometimes come to Earth. Obviously, where I am the Dean of Schomolance Academy, the masquerading class is very believable at being whatever they pretend to be."

Changing the subject, the devil says, "Now are we getting prepared to listen to Lust's presentation tomorrow? Making sure we understand everything."

Penny looks at him and says, "Yes sir, no problem whatsoever, I intend to be up on every topic, so that I can deliver it if necessary. Don't you worry. I know not to rely on other demons. I always make sure I can do it all myself and do it better than they can. We never know when something's going to go wrong, with one of them."

The devil looks at her, and smiles, and says, "Excellent, I knew I could count on you, Penny. I see a lot of myself in you. Now skedaddle."

Penny heads back to her dorm.

———

The devil looks upward to Heaven and says, "You're not getting her. I don't care who you send down here. You're not getting Penny. She is my pride."

Penny walks across the campus to her dorm. It's a small room, with a wardrobe, a desk, a little refrigerator, and a bed. It's not much. It's just enough for one to sleep and study. She walks in, puts her stuff on the desk, lays down on the bed, and lets out a big exhale.

———

'THE DEVIL SEEMED TO like me, so that's good. Now, I've got to prepare for tomorrow, after I take a little nap. Apparently even demons can get overwhelmed by emotions. Oh does this mean I'm becoming mortal. Is this what happens when you take on the mortal form? You get all their feelings and emotions, that's inconvenient. At any rate, this demon, whether in mortal form or anything else, needs a nap after this day.

Chapter 3 Details

The devil walks into the lecture hall and immediately, he is confronted by angry demons. They just about jump out of their seats, with a ton of questions. The first question is from Wrath. "What the hell is going on with us? Why am I so limited in my physical abilities? What is this crap?"

The devil just gives a smile and says, "Oh you're talking about the limits on your powers. Yeah sorry, I figured the easiest way to have you learn how to tempt mortals is to make you mortal. So you not only don't have your powers, you essentially are mortal. You can die, but you already know where you're going. Ironically, I am in the details and yet, conveniently forget to mention them.

"Let's face it, you're trying to catch the mortals, so I'm giving you all their limitations, that means you're going to need to eat like a mortal would need to eat. You're going to have to go to the bathroom, like a mortal would have to go to the bathroom. You're going to have sexual desires, like a mortal would have sexual desires. The whole gambit of all those feelings. You're going to want more, like they want more. My personal favorite, you're going to hear what you want to hear and see what you want to see. Eventually it's going to drive you nuts, but my whole goal is to have a group of elite demons, who can get souls. Know thy enemy, know thyself.

"It's kind of like when God sent his only beloved son down to Earth. I, essentially, did the same thing. I've just sent you UP to Earth, instead of down to Earth. You are going to have to learn, what these mortals have to deal with. So yeah sorry about that. Well I'm not really sorry. It's kind of fun for me. I get to watch all of you deal with all the crap the mortals have to deal with. Basically the rules are don't die and give your speech. Really shouldn't be all that difficult."

"Why were we able to go into people's thoughts yesterday and have powers during class?" asks Wrath.

"When you are in this class, you have all your powers or rather I can help you maintain your powers," replies the devil. "You are actually up on Earth, on a regular college campus. People can see you, so yeah, you're very exposed. You are at risk of death. The other demons down at Schomolance Academy have their powers and are not at risk of death."

The demons are not happy.

Envy asks "How is this possible? We are demons. We were never alive, so we cannot die."

"Well it's too late to change your mind now, so, I guess this doesn't matter. It's just like when I got to torture Job or tempt Jesus, sometimes God allows me to try things. This time, I get to make a handful of you mortal. I put a small number of demons at risk and in exchange, I get better demons."

Sloth asks, "what's our risk?"

The devil smiles as he answers, "Technically, if you die while mortal, you get judged and likely sent to Hell. Instead of being the torturer, you would be the tortured. Sorry, should I have told you? Explicitly mentioning details, again, not what I'm known for."

The class looks at the devil dumbfounded. They didn't know so much was at risk.

"If we aren't chosen as the lead soul catcher, do the rest of us die and become tortured, or do the rest of us get to go back to where we were in Hell, like do we lose our rank. Is it soul catcher or bust?" asks Gluttony.

"No, if you're not selected and you don't die, while here on Earth, you go back to your ranks in Hell," says the devil.

"How do we know we can trust you? How do we know no more details are just going to be brought up or remembered or explained?" says Gluttony.

"Well, you can't. I'm the devil. You can't ever really trust me. You're a demon, can anyone ever really trust you?" asks the devil.

Wrath says, "Back to me, I have a few more questions about this whole mortal mess. I was in the middle of screaming and yelling at someone and suddenly I got tired. I'm Wrath. I don't get tired."

Penny says, "You think that's bad. I was about to start studying and then I began to worry, to the point I was tired! I can't get tired, how can I get tired and still study more than everybody else.

"You know for me to have to study and worry about things like I want to put this here and that there. It's exhausting. I needed to take a nap. I don't take naps. I have a million and one things to do and apparently collapsing on the bed is now one of them. Also I am now apparently a neurotic mess, so that's lovely. I'm sure I'm real fun to be around."

Sloth laughs and says, "Penny, you weren't that much fun to be around before. I, for one, am totally ok with this needing to take a nap thing."

Despair quietly speaks for the first time and says, "I'm ok with the whole human experience. I fit into that pretty well."

Gluttony stops cramming potato chips into his mouth long enough to say, "At least the food is not too bad up here and their portions are huge. I am so glad we ended up in America. I would hate to be in one of those survival type countries. We pretty much landed in the land of gluttony."

"I'd say we landed in the land of everything and everyone wanting everything else," Envy said.

Wrath says to the devil, "So that's it. We're just kind of stuck with mortal limitations, until, how long is this class gonna go on for?"

The devil looks and says, "just until the end of the semester. I figure we're here on Earth, you might as well learn all you can about the mortals. Those are whose souls we want to catch.

"Once you are back into Hell and just coming up sporadically as needed, you go back to your full demon powers. So this isn't forever, calm down.

"While you are here on Earth and in this regular college, I'm going to need you to not reveal who we are. I've already gotten chased out of Transylvania. I was chased out of Salem. Although strangely, the tourism boards want me back. I guess, I'm good for business. Anyway, I am sick and tired of having everyone be on their guard. My whole jam was to pretend that I don't exist, that was my greatest trick. It kind of loses the trick when everybody knows to look for you.

"Like I said, if we went up to people in our full form and said follow me. They'd crap themselves and run to the nearest church, with the whole bless me father for I have sinned. We don't need that nonsense. I want to very slowly, inch by inch, get them to commit a whole lot of sins, so that they can go to Hell. This shouldn't be difficult.

"So sorry, you are stuck in your mortal form until this class and selection process is over.

"Now if you all don't mind, we're going to be getting back to class."

Chapter 4 Lust

The devil calls for Lust to come to the front of the room and join him.

Lust, represented by a beautiful woman dressed in a tight red velvet dress, with black stockings, gets up and seductively moves her way to the front of the lecture hall and sits on the devil's lap. Her dress has a slit on the side revealing her thigh high stockings. Everyone has their eyes set on her. She knows it and she loves it. She exudes sensuality.

After she sits on the professor's lap, she gives him a wet, open-mouth kiss, and says "hi" in a very breathy voice.

She addresses the class. "I'm Lust. I'm desire. I am not passion. Passion is reserved for when you're working for something good. Something you care about. I don't care about you or the mortals. I care about one thing. I want someone's soul. I guess now I want two things because I also want that position of lead soul catcher."

Lust smiles a coy smile and continues speaking. "No, I don't care about you or any of the mortals. Oh and to make this speech easier, I am just going to say 'you' when I mean any of the mortals. After all, we're all mortal right now.

"Back to my speech. I just want you and well, everybody to look at me; and want me; and you do, at least while you are in your mortal form. The mortals all want me, as well.

"Now please understand, lust can be a very strong desire for anything, it's usually sex. It's like gluttony is usually food, but not always. So how do I use lust to collect my souls? It's very simple.

"You all stopped what you were doing to look at me and that's what I want you to do. I am here to interrupt your thoughts. I am here to make you take notice.

"I'm wearing very tight clothes that make you look at me a little longer than perhaps you should. You want to run your hands all over my body and I understand that. I applaud that. I want that. So, here are the good things you want it, I want it, let's do it. How do I then damn you to Hell, which is my end game?

"At the end of the day, I'm a deadly sin. I'm a totally good sin. We are going to have so much fun, for a little while. But, ultimately, I'm a deadly sin, and I want your soul.

"First off upon seeing me, I have your undivided attention. I can assure you, you are not looking at or thinking about any other human being. You are solely thinking about yourself and what you want to do to me. You're not thinking about how that will destroy your spouse's trust in you and bring their world crashing down. All you're thinking about is how you're going to feel good in the short term, which is what I want. I'm here for your soul. I'm not here to convince you that I love you. I don't care about you. This essentially is what lust is and what I represent. I have you so busy worrying about yourself and what you want that you don't even have a moment to think about what everyone else wants or what everyone else needs. I have separated you from everyone else. Jesus Christ wants you to remember your fellow man, but I'm going to make you forget about your fellow man."

It's at this moment, when everyone else in the room is hanging on Lust's every word; that the devil goes into the head of Despair. The devil, while in Despair's head, plants the idea, *don't worry, you'll never be her. It's never expected of you, which is kind of good, because you wouldn't be able to have everyone want you.*

Despair looks down at herself and realizes, *I'm never going to be this person. I'm never going to be the object of someone's desire. No one's ever going to look at me and think "yay I get to be with this person."*

Very quickly, Penny, looks at Lust and thinks *my goodness, I'm pretty intellectual and even I am thinking about the flesh side of my body. She just makes you want to look at her.*

Lust says, "I am lack of connection, lack of love, and ultimate desire that can never be filled.

"Well tell me professor, did I do good? Did I make everyone forget about everything, but my body, and wanting me?"

With that, the devil looks at Lust and says, "Oh Lust, trust me, everyone was looking at you. You had everyone's attention, which is what I sculpted you for."

The devil turns his attention back to the class. "All right kids, here's how we use lust to gather people's souls. Obviously, if you are worried about or satisfying your earthly desires, you are not thinking about your fellow man.

"I'm not trying to make small or light of the following problems. I love problems. I'm not trying to solve them, at all. I want to create more. I'm now getting all sides of the argument. The mortals can't win, but I can.

"Let's consider the ramifications of the mortals actions. Mortals never do. So someone should and we are all about ramifications.

"Lets bring up a male mortal, that was recently sent to Hell. I can list off the ramifications. I'll bring in a female later. Humans hate it when you only pick on one gender. See, I'm fair."

A man appears looking confused. He sees Lust and smiles. She waves and blows him a kiss.

The devil looks at the mortal and says to him, "Ok, you were a naughty boy. We are now going to list at least some of the consequences of your actions."

The man looked at the devil with a puzzled expression.

The devil answered his look back with a quick eye roll. "All right, real quick. You're dead. I'm the devil. This is a class about lust. Now here is a list of some of the things that sent you to Hell."

The man's eyes rolled into the back of his head and he started to sway. The devil looked over to him and quickly said "There is no passing out in Hell. Literally, you can't. You will still remain conscious. Otherwise, it's cheating."

The devil now looks at a clip board and says, "Ok, now you had an affair. That is the big sin, but now it is time to look at all the ramifications. Class, pay attention to these. Man acts without thinking of the ramifications he will have to deal with in the future. When he starts to suffer the consequences of his actions; then he realizes what he has done. Then he questions how anyone could love him, never mind, forgive him. Now, he is more and more separated from Christ, and that is our opening."

The devil then begins to list bullet points on the board.

"Ok the ramifications of an affair:

1. Loss of trust- The wife is just emotionally destroyed. The person who was supposed to be her rock, her safe harbor, just gut punched her

2. Disease to wife. She now has an assortment of diseases and is humiliated to have every medical worker know she was either cheated on or sleeps around.

3. Destroy happy home. Let's face it, no one is happy. The wife's happy home is destroyed. The kids no longer have the home they always knew. The mistress likely has been kicked to the curb, in the vain hope by the man, that all can be made right.

4. Pregnancy -The mistress is pregnant. She, now, has even more to deal with. No matter what she chooses it will have a major impact on her life.

5. Children born of the affair will be effected. They may blame themselves for destroying a happy home. Even though it couldn't have been that happy, if he had an affair. There would also likely be an absentee father.

6. Divorce

7. Child support for both families

8. No money because he has to pay all the judgements, any time he does get visitation, all the kids hate him.

9. Deal with mistress

The devil then looks at the man he brought up from hell and says, "Ok, I'm done with you for the purpose of this class. Back to Hell." The man disappears in a puff of smoke, with a look of horror and bewilderment.

"Before we get into anything else let me explain what we're looking at. The big question will be; does the man think he is worthy of forgiveness. I don't care whether he could be forgiven. I care about whether he feels he is worthy of forgiveness, that's where we collect our souls. I don't need you to be guilty, I just need you to think you are.

"The Bible pretty much says in Mark 3:28-30, that Jesus says that all sins can be forgiven, except for blasphemy against the Holy Spirit. The Holy Spirit lives in all who believe, and rejecting it means rejecting the love of God and sacrifice of Jesus Christ.

The devil interprets his recount of scripture and says, "So if you don't believe someone can forgive you, then you can't be forgiven."

The devil continues, "even better these aren't my rules. I am damning them by their own rules. It's even better, they are damning themselves. The mortals often think surely Christ couldn't possibly love me after all I've done."

"Now, we get to the other side. The woman's point of view because the mortals would go nuts if I didn't bring up the other gender. So, let's bring the mistress up from Hell, shall we?"

This time a woman appears and looks at the devil with a puzzled expression.

The devil answered her look with a quick eye roll. "Again, really? All right, real quick. You're dead. I'm the devil. This is a class about lust. Now here is a list of some of the things that sent you to Hell."

"You are, or were, the pregnant mistress. This is going to be damn confusing with switching tenses, so I'm just going to speak for you. Really dear, I couldn't do a worse job with your life than you did. I mean let's face it you were sent to Hell. Well, right now, you're in a class, but you'll be going back to Hell."

The woman then looks over to the devil, with a terrified and overwhelmed look on her face. The devil then sends the woman back to Hell in another puff of smoke, and for a brief moment the class can hear all the shrieks and screams from Hell.

The devil continues his lecture and says , "The mistress thinks 'Oh well now I've got to eat better, if I am keeping the baby. On the other hand, people have fought tooth and nail for my legal right to end this pregnancy.'"

The devil continues, "I can plant little ideas in her head. 'You weren't ready to be a mother. The father is an adulterer. You know that because you're the one he had an affair with. You are going to have to go through the court system and prove that he's the one you slept with and get a court order of how much money he's going to pay you every month. You have heard all the rumors about how hard it is to be a single mother. Now, they have all these things out about "shout out your abortion." You don't have to feel bad about it. It is totally socially okay."

The devil looks at the class, to make sure they are following along. He wants to make sure they know, he doesn't judge. He doesn't care about the mortals, so he doesn't care what they do.

He just sets traps and otherwise looks for openings for people to not believe they are forgivable.

The devil continues, "Never mind that you're going to carry the decision, of whether or not to keep the baby, in your mind for the rest of your life. There may not be any legal barriers. Let's say best case scenario, no legal barriers whatsoever. It's not even physically difficult for you to get there or afford the procedure. Let's assume all the medical stuff works out great, so you no longer have the problem of the child. You can concentrate on your work and you don't have to worry about it.

"It's as if it never existed. The problem is, late at night, when no one's around, I'll know it existed. You have given me one more thing to torment you with. I will be the cause of one more sleepless night. I will extract tears from you.

"You'll cry. I'll make sure of it and also I will lead you to believe Jesus Christ could never love someone, who committed such an act. No matter how much it was legally allowed. Even if people are telling you 'don't worry, it's morally okay. We are shouting out, how good it is, you did not have to be a single mother. In fact, it is good, the child didn't have to grow up in poverty. You did a good thing.'

"For some reason, no one wants to hear, this is a bad thing. No one wants to listen to the fact that this will weigh on your mind later. You may not believe it, but quietly in the night when you think no one's listening, you're going to remember. That's what I love. All I need is some little thing to convince you that Jesus doesn't love you.

"You don't have to work very hard at this because no mortal really thinks they're worthy of Christ's love. As long as, I got the mortal in that endless Hell loop, where I have separated them from Christ's love, then I have my inroad. The mortals barely believe he exists, never mind that whole - love and forgiveness thing. If a mortal feels worthy of forgiveness, my job is that much harder because then they could be saved. But and here is the big thing. I'm not here to make friends. I'm not here to do, what is in the mortal's best interest. I'm here for their soul."

Penny raises her hand.

The devil looks at her and says "Penny, my pride, what is it darling?"

"Okay I have heard you talk about the guys and the girls, on the complications surrounding abortion. I know you don't take sides. You're just here for the conflict, but it kind of seems like you are pro-life. Am I missing something?" Penny asks.

"No, you can be on both sides of the argument. I have a lot of fun collecting the souls of Pro-Lifers.

"If they think, they're holier than everyone else, then that's the sin of pride. They aren't loving their fellow man.

"Penny, you should have seen this one coming. It's a pride problem," the devil says. Penny nods in agreement, somewhat ashamed that she missed something so obvious.

"I can collect from one side just as easy as I can collect from the other side. Remember, I just want to win, I don't care who loses, as long as I win, that's all that matters to me.

"I'm breaking the world up into us versus them. As long as there's an us versus them going on. There is no we. Christ wants WE. I don't want we. I want ME.

"Also, there were other contenders to being a deadly sin. Some call it the 8th or 9th deadly sin. I just need it to be a sin and preferably a deadly sin. One such sin is despair."

HE WHO DOES NOT EXIST

With this Despair looks up, almost hopeful, almost. She thinks, *Maybe the devil will talk to me directly. Maybe, I'll get to talk to the class and explain why I'm here and why I matter.*

The devil looks dismissively at her and shakes his head no and continues lecturing.

"The other sin is sophisticated cowardice. You have a good argument, but lack the courage to do the right thing.

"Many pro lifers fall into this category. God doesn't want the mortals to bomb abortion clinics. He is all about love and that is not love. They should not scare the mother. We can get the bombers.

"Some people do it the right way. Some offer help. They arrange for the mothers to go to doctors and offer assistance, like who to get in contact with, if the mothers want to put the child up for adoption. They offer programs that can help with food, for mother and child. They basically help set the mother and child up for success, whatever that may look like. We usually can't get those people, unless they've done something else. We can always dream.

"Remember what I said at the start of this lecture. I'm not trying to make small or light of the problems. I love problems. I'm not trying to solve them, at all. I want to create more. I'm now getting multiple sides of the issue. They can't win, but I can."

———

Greetings reader, I wanted to make sure you were still paying attention. Things are about to get interesting. Remember mortals only hear what they want to hear and see what they want to see.

Chapter 5 First Encounter

Penny walks into her dorm room. In there, is the girl from the cafeteria. Immediately, Penny drops all her things onto the floor and screams.

The girl stares back and says, "Hi, we've been talking about you and I wanted to meet you."

"I'm sorry, you talk about me? Who are you? Why are you talking about me?" says Penny.

"Ok, this will sound weird, but I'm an angel."

"What do you mean, you're an angel?" says Penny.

"I mean, (pointing upward), I'm one of them. We've been watching you. I thought it would be fun to come down and say hi. Hi!" The angel gives a little wave.

Penny looks at the angel in utter disbelief and says, "Ok, you're an angel?"

The angel says, "That really shouldn't shock you. You're a demon. An angel visiting a demon is kind of odd, but the existence of an angel shouldn't shock you. I mean you're a demon. Did you think there were only demons in the world? Angels exist too. We just don't make a big fuss about it."

The angel then looks at Penny and says, "Could I sit down? I'm a little tired. It's been a long journey."

Penny walks over and picks her belongings up off the floor. She puts everything on her desk. She turns to the angel and says, "What do you want, angel? You're here. Why are you here?" Penny is acting tough. Her defenses are up.

"Oh, we're very interested in you. We are interested in demons being temporarily mortal. So, I thought it would be nice to see, who you are."

"What do you mean you guys talk about me?"

"Well that's about it. We occasionally look at the newly promoted department head demons. You know, to see what we're up against. You stood out. We, kind of thought, it'd be fun to see who is going to be the new lead soul catcher."

Penny looks at the angel. "Do you know for certain, I'm going to be the new lead soul catcher?"

"No, no, no. Just a hunch."

Penny says, "Oh well then, you're not of much help to me. Also, I'm not going to get to be lead soul catcher, unless, I hit the books. Not that this whole conversation isn't exceedingly interesting, but I've got work to do."

"Ok, just know, you're probably never really alone. I know, you know, the devil can get into your thoughts on Earth, but so can the angels. All that he can do, we can do, except we usually do it for good, whereas, he usually is not doing it for good."

Penny looks at the angel and says, "Oh. Makes sense. I mean whatever we, demons, can do; you, angels, can do. Ok this has been a lot of new information. I have notes from class to review. I understand you took a big long trip, but I need time to digest this. What am I supposed to do with this new information?"

The angel looks at her, with a tired look, and says, "I don't know. I hadn't thought that far. I just wanted to see, who you were; what you're doing; what you're about; and all that other stuff.

"Basically, I'm not spying on you, I'm not collecting information for any specific purpose. I wasn't sent to observe you. No one sent me, I came on my own."

Penny says, "That's great, I need a minute to digest all this. Is there a way I can contact you, like a phone number."

"Oh, you can't. This is kind of a one way thing. I can appear to you. You can't make me appear. I'm always here, listening, though. If you just say 'hey angel' I'll respond. Well, at least for awhile."

Penny says, "Ok then angel, why don't you go? I'm going to review my notes from today's lecture and prepare for tomorrow's lecture."

The angel looks at her and says, "That's ok. I totally understand. By the way, I know you're going to go and tell the other demons. I am totally cool with it. You're allowed, not a problem. They might not believe you, because, let's face it, they didn't believe you, when I was sitting in the same room.

"Demons can rarely see angels. The angel has to want to be seen; or not be able to be invisible; and the viewer must believe in the angel's existence. Same with mortals. Some mortals can see us and some can't. It's complicated. I'm still working on the visibility part. I'm a young angel, like you're a young demon. You know learning all the ins and outs. Ok well with that, I'm gonna go. I'll drop in later."

Penny closes the door behind the angel and slumps to the floor. Penny thinks to herself, '*Ok I just saw an angel. I just talked to an angel, not that weird, I mean I am a demon. I guess I always knew the other side existed. I just wasn't prepared to meet one.'*

Penny shakes her head and just sits on the floor quietly, for a few minutes. She is letting everything seep into her mortal brain. She hates being in mortal form. She could do so much more if she was allowed to have all her powers.

While all this is going on, there's a knock at her door. She gets up from the floor and opens the door. Standing there is the devil.

"Hi, Sir," says Penny.

"Is everything ok?" he says looking around her dorm room.

Penny says "The weirdest thing just happened. When I walked into my room, there was someone in here waiting for me."

The devil looked a little concerned. He said, "Oh really and who was it bothering my poor Penny?"

"She wasn't really bothering me. She was just here. She said she was an angel."

The devil kind of chuckles, looks at Penny, and says, "Do you believe her?"

"I don't know. This entire thing just kinda threw me for a loop. I guess, I knew angels had to exist. I mean we exist. The whole equilibrium thing. I got it. There have to be the opposites. You're going to have sweet. You're going to have salty. I got it – Ying Yang. I just never thought it through and now, that just happened. I was about to review my notes from Lust's lecture."

"Ah yes, that was a fun little lecture, wasn't it?"

Penny replies, "Yes, yes it was. Anyhow, I'm going to prepare for tomorrow's lecture. I just might take a nap, first. Being mortal is hard. It was so much easier, when we weren't mortal and didn't have all these feelings, like fear and confusion."

"I have to leave you as a mortal while you're on Earth, for the selection process. It wouldn't be fair, if one of you got to have all your powers and the other ones didn't. I need to have all of you learn, what it's like to be mortal. What it's like, to deal with all these things."

"I understand. I don't need and I am not looking for any special treatment," Penny says, looking confused, scared, and indignant.

The devil says, "All righty, well, I'll let you take your nap. I'm pretty sure you need one right now. You have a lot running around in your mind. I will see you tomorrow morning for class.

"Penny, don't give a single thought to this angel. Let's face it, there's a lot of weird people running around. There's a department, in Hell, whose whole purpose is to imitate other people. Pull the wool over other people's eyes. You know, wolf in sheep's clothing and all that."

Penny is immediately relieved and says, "I took everything she said at face value. Okay I'm gonna go take that nap now."

The devil says, "Goodnight. Don't worry, I'm sure your notes and understanding of Lust's lecture are great. Gluttony's lecture is tomorrow. I am sure that will be interesting or that we can at least stay awake for it. All right, talk to you later."

With that Penny closes the door and sits on her bed, with her head in her hands. She thinks, *Ok I may have seen an angel, which I hadn't before, but makes sense because I'm a demon and I exist. Or I've seen some one from the Schomolance masquerading class, which I myself have taken before. I know how to change forms, make people think I'm your friend when I'm not. I know how to do the whole wolf in sheep's clothing thing. I didn't get that sense from this angel, but maybe she's better at it than I was. Not that anybody's better at anything than me. I mean I am the best of the best. I just didn't get that feeling with her.'*

'I've either met someone better at being a demon than I am, which really isn't possible, or ...

Penny then stopped thinking and just began talking out loud to herself. "Come on, Penny, this is just self doubt talk. In fact, it's likely one of the other demons trying to get into my head!

"That's exactly what's going on. The other demons, my competition, all know I'm under a lot of pressure and they thought let's throw Penny off her game, and knock her out of the competition for lead soul catcher. That's it.

"It is either Avarice, Wrath, or Envy. It wouldn't be Sloth, that would require too much effort. Lust thinks sleeping with the devil is enough. Gluttony probably hasn't given me, or any one else, a single thought.

"I think it is Avarice. He said how much he wants to be lead soul catcher. He said he will do what he needs to do to be lead soul catcher. He probably thinks what he needs to do is throw me off my game. He probably saw me as the biggest threat."

Penny is now up and pacing as she talks out her deductions. "Avarice saw me as a big threat and he said, 'Ok how will I throw Penny off her game. I'm going to pretend I'm an angel. I won't cause any problems and I'll just sit there while good old

Penny looks and thinks she sees me in the cafeteria. Later on, I'll just show up in her room and again tell her 'I'm an angel. I'm always here. You can't even get in touch with me. If you want me, you can just say 'Hey angel.' He probably couldn't even think of an angel's name.

"Yeah that's what's going on and even worse I made myself look like an idiot in front of the devil. Why couldn't I tell him I had already seen through Avarice's plan.

"Let's face it, if it was Lust, she would try to corrupt me in my mortal body by trying to seduce me. So I can rule her out.

"Avarice is highly probable. Sloth wouldn't have put any effort into it. I just don't see Envy as a big go getter. Not worried about Despair, she wouldn't have wanted to risk getting caught and I don't see her striving for anything.

"I think, I'm just tired. I can't even name everyone. This is stupid. It could be Wrath. It would be odd for it to be Wrath, still it could be Wrath, but unlikely, it's more likely Avarice. Sloth couldn't give a crap. Envy wouldn't take that much action; she'd want the result, but she wouldn't take the action necessary to get the result. Gluttony, I don't know, I- I just don't think so. I think, yeah, I think that's it. It's Avarice. I'll yell at him, tomorrow.

"This is too much. I am now understanding the mortal thing completely. This whole mortal form thing sucks. I want my powers back."

'I'm going to take a nap now', with that she flops onto her bed and falls asleep.

———

The devil is standing outside Penny's room in the hall and he knows all that just went through her mind. He is furious and yells up to the sky, "Ok, I didn't think you were going to come down and suddenly mess with one of my demons. I like Penny. As you know, pride holds a special place in my heart. Why are we bothering my pride, my Penny? Why are we bothering my pride with an angel? It's not like you're getting her. She's mine. I get to keep her. You can't have her.

Oh, this is a little game. You want to see if you can take a demon from the devil. Well your not taking any demons from the devil, most certainly not Penny. She's mine. Don't go messing with my pride."

The angel appears in front of the devil. "You knew the risk of bringing the demons to Earth and making them mortal. They are fair game."

"Don't mess with Penny," the devil says, with a firm conviction. He is concerned. The other side had never tried to take one of his demons. He always knew it was a risk, though.

Chapter 6 Avarice

Penny walks into the lecture hall, right up to Avarice, and says, "Ok, nice try yesterday, trying to throw me off my game? Are you that scared of me?"

Avarice looks at Penny and says, "I have no idea what you're talking about. Has the pressure of all this just gotten to you? I haven't seen you, since Lust's lecture yesterday and I'm not at all worried about you. Never have been."

Avarice continues, "You are just trying to throw me off my game on my presentation day. That's pathetic, I expected more from you. Now, why don't you watch and learn from one of the big boy demons."

"What do you mean it's your presentation day? Gluttony is supposed to go today."

The devil turns to Penny and says, "Oh sorry dear, we've done a little change in the schedule. You know details, I love them, but mentioning them, not my strong point"

The devil addresses the class. "Yesterday's little presentation by Lust was fantastically wonderful. I don't know about the rest of you, but I was certainly satisfied. Now, we have a slight change in the order of speakers. Instead of Gluttony, it's going to be Avarice speaking to us today. Gluttony asked for the change. Avarice said he was happy to make his presentation today. So with that, take it away."

Avarice stands up and walks toward the front of the lecture hall. He is a handsome man dressed in a nice suit. He flashes a perfect smile. The girl demons are staring at him, gushing, even Penny has to admit he is good looking.

"As you know, I am Avarice. I am heightened levels of greed. You can never get enough of me. I am like that first line of cocaine, you want more and you will never again achieve the high you get from that first line. Doesn't matter to me though, once you have tasted a little bit, your mine. Oh and I like Lust's idea, so I may say, "the mortals" or I may say "you" because hey, we're all mortal now, or at least for a little while.

"There is a famous line in the movie, "Wall Street", that 'greed is good'. I love that sentiment. It's true for me, greed is good, well for all the demons greed is good, we get lots of people into Hell with that one. I mean you think about it, who doesn't want more. There's always a certain basic amount that everybody needs, but we go a bit above and beyond.

"There is a bible verse the mortals always get wrong. They think it is money is the root of all evil. It is in the King James version chapter 1 Timothy 6:10 "For the love of money is the root of all evil..."

"The love of money is the root of all evil. You aren't supposed to love money. You're supposed to love your fellow man. I want to get in the way of that whole love thy fellow man. I want to be that small wedge that starts to separate you from Jesus.

"I have to tell you a fun story of one of the best people I got into Hell. When this man was a young child, he grew up poor. I mean really poor. He did not know where his next meal was coming from. In the slums of India, he worked his little tail off. Eventually after a lot of hard work and a lot of education, he was worth hundreds of millions, but it wasn't enough. Honestly if you have the love of money, you can never have enough.

"So I kept saying to him, we'll make a little more. I already knew how to put little thoughts in people's minds. On our first day, I just acted like it was new information to me. I'm a demon. I don't play fair. Now back to our greedy little man from India.

"I continued to remind him: 'Oh those people have more than you, why don't you have what they have?' Here's the problem. Once you get people thinking 'why don't I have what they have.' They then think I'll get there with just a little more work.

"They have a list of who's the richest person. Does it really matter which one is the richest person? Once you get to a certain dollar amount, do you really care whether you have the most toys? I loved that '80s expression of 'he who has the most toys wins.' Truly, that is greed personified. I love it.

"So here's what happened to that rich guy, who used to live on the streets. I got him to run a large stock market scam. He went to jail. He really wanted to have a billion dollars. He created a big scheme and still never reached the billionaire status. He went to jail and lost everything he worked hard for. He screwed over lots and lots of people, lots of misery, lots of fortunes lost. It was a great day for demons.

"So let me explain why greed is bad or why it's so easy to be converted over to our side. The reason greed is a sin is simple. It comes down to, you can't have two masters. If you love money, and I mean love money. You lust after money. I was paying attention to Lust's lecture yesterday, of course, who wasn't." He then stares at Lust for a minute, daydreaming, before pulling himself back together and addressing the class. Meanwhile, she smiles at him and gives a little wink.

"Right, so, you can't have two masters. If money is your master, Jesus is not. This guy, who was the pauper in India, didn't care about his fellow man. He screwed over his fellow man. He wanted more. I love when people want more. Too much is never enough.

"Now, let's talk about the average person. You know, someone who isn't a billionaire. Let's talk about credit cards. Right now, those interest rates are as high as 36% per year, compounding daily. The mortals do not read the fine print, nor understand compound interest. We can charge what we want and we do.

"So, let's give people a credit card. I'm going to put a 30% interest rate. To lure the mortals in, I'll give them an introductory rate of 5.99%. Hell, I could give the mortals an introductory rate of 0%. Either way, I win, they lose.

"The majority of the mortals don't pay the balance off every month. The majority also do not pay it off by the end of the introductory period. The interest is going to be charged retroactively. The devil wins, under my system, and the mortals lose.

"We're not done playing. Oh and did I say 30% interest, I should have said 29.97%, so you think you're getting this great deal of a 29% interest rate. I don't know why, but for some reason, mortals round down.

"This will lead to crippling debt. This will lead the mortals to commit almost any sin to get out from under the debt. Even better, they will feel like the credit card companies are to blame for them being in debt, even though they signed their names. They even enjoyed their purchases."

The devil gives a slow clap and says, "Wow, I am the devil and even I am impressed."

Avarice smiles, nods, and continues, "Thank you, that's just one part of my plan to get more people desperate and put themselves in a position where they're ready to send themselves to Hell.

"Now I wonder what would be the best thing to talk about next. I can either explain credit scores, payday loans, or bankruptcy. The credit score one is quick and it can lead to enough fear that I can get a mortal started in our direction.

"So I have this system of imaginary scores. Mortals like scores. They like to rank themselves. I call these credit scores. It lets mortals know how good someone is at repaying debt. I use basically completely made up numbers. The score even goes from like 300 to 850. I don't even use 0 to 100. A scoring system that would make sense. So the higher you score, then the lower the interest rate, and the easier your life is. The lower your score, then the higher your interest rate is, and the easier my job, as a demon going after your soul, is. My goal is to get you to Hell. You start missing payments and I start smiling.

"With the crazy FICO credit score I can justify charging higher interest rates. With the higher interest rates, I get more of your money. You have less money to pay the debts you owe and then I only need one or two little things to go wrong. The mortals make it so that if things don't go perfectly, their whole balancing act falls apart.

"When this happens, as it often does, they have to file bankruptcy. Now with the bankruptcy laws, many people get to keep most of their stuff. Except they are poor, so most of their stuff is crap. If they owned appreciating assets; they probably wouldn't be in this situation. They usually owe more than the car is worth. They usually owe more than the house is worth. There really isn't anything for creditors to take. You basically take a poor person, make them feel bad for being poor, and charge them for being poor.

"This whole process of course justifies my lowering their credit score. Since they have a lower credit score, they feel bad about themselves, and I can use that to my advantage.

"I mail them a letter. It explains I know they are a credit risk. I know they filed bankruptcy. I am willing to take a risk on them because I think they're worth it. These idiot mortals feel so bad and so guilty for having had to file bankruptcy; that, they are just thankful someone will take a risk on them. There is no risk to me.

"Let me explain how this works. I lend them $1,000 at 35% interest compounding daily. They rack up $1,000. Eventually, as in about 8 years down the road, they can't pay the money back. That little debt of $1,000 is now worth over $16,000. Now it's true, I'm out $1,000, but during this time, they've been paying me interest, on interest, on interest, and so on. So when I have to write off $1,000 and remove it off my tax profits. I have already profited off them, tremendously. I am fine. Now, this is your second bankruptcy and you're going to feel horrible and I'm going to use that to my advantage.

"Now the mortal, not wanting to risk a credit card, or not able to get a credit card, and not knowing any other way, goes down, and gets a payday loan. Folks there is no way, even I, could come up with something this bad. That was cooked up by the boys in research and development in the accounting department of Hell. They outdid themselves. This can get up to one thousand percent interest. Even I'm amazed at how quickly someone can get trapped and can't get out.

In short, the mortals write a post dated check for the amount they want to borrow plus the finance charges. The future date on the check is written for approximately the date of the next direct deposit of their paycheck. Now I don't have to tell you that things come up. Let's face it, that's how we collect souls. The people doing payday loans do not have savings for anything that might come up. They usually don't have budgets. So, it really doesn't take much for the mortals to very quickly have to go back to the payday loan people and postdate them a new check for the new loan amount because they can't have the original amount taken out of their account. They don't have extra money. If they did, they wouldn't be going to a payday loan place.

Avarice speaks to the devil directly, "Basically that's greed summarized and my plan to bring us, as many desperate mortals as we can, into Hell. I want to be your go-to demon. I want that role as lead soul catcher, where I get to work directly for you."

Avarice points to himself and says, "I love money," points to the devil says "You're the root of all evil. Tell me what else I need to do, to be lead soul catcher."

Penny leans over to Despair and says, "Wow, ok talk about not having any pride. He doesn't even care that he's screwing people over and way to beg for a job. I don't know. I think he's just going a little over the top."

Avarice over hears the comment and says, "Penny, you are a deadly sin. You do know, your job is to try to be the devil's protégé. That's why we're in the class. You are supposed to be advocating for yourself. You are supposed to be the best demon.

Penny says, "I take pride in what I do. I am above all of you. I don't have to sink to your level. I can be above all of this and still do an excellent job."

The devil now moves himself into Despair's thoughts. *It's ok to hear you might not be as smart as Penny, Avarice, or even Lust. I bet if you try real hard you will get the point of the lecture, maybe not. Keep trying and keep beating yourself up over it. Sooner or later, it will get into that thick skull of yours. Just keep at it, over and over again, keep thinking you're not good enough. It almost seems like we've been here before.*

Penny raises her hand and asks, "I have a question. What's the difference between lust and avarice and envy? It seems like they're all kind of intertwined."

The devil answers, "Well that's simple. Lust is a strong desire. Envy is also a strong desire, but it's a desire of not wanting others to be better than you or not have more.

"Lust is fine with everybody in the room having a good time. Avarice is fine with everybody desiring something and getting what they desire. Envy is not. Envy wants to have better than every one else. Avarice is ok with wanting money and wanting everything. Yes, they do kind of want to be at the top of the food chain. That is what they keep working for and they know they'll never get to the top of the food chain. Here is the big difference, most of the deadly sins for a brief shining moment, enjoy the crap out of whatever they get.

"Whereas, envy is forever reaching and comparing. You can never really arrive because only one person gets to be the best and there will always be someone better and envy will make sure you forever chase that person. You truly never arrive. Not being on top of that list or any list, takes away any joy the mortals get from the big house or driving off the lot in a new car. There is always something better or newer. Basically there's never a moment that envy enjoys anything."

"Am I making sense Penny?" the devil says.

Penny kind of nods yes. "I understand what you're saying." Even though part of her was also thinking *this a lot to take in.*

Penny, then says, loud enough for the devil to hear. "All right Despair, are you ready to get lunch?" Penny makes quick eye contact with the devil.

"I don't know," answers Despair. She both wants and doesn't want to be with the group for lunch.

"Come on we're mortals, we got to eat and besides, I want chocolate," says Penny.

Chapter 7 Second Encounter

All of the demons are seated in the cafeteria. In front of Lust is a piece of chocolate cake. She leans over to Penny and says, "Can I tempt you with some chocolate cake?"

Penny takes a bite off Lust's fork, while it was still in Lust's hands. Immediately, Penny feels wrong, just wrong. There is nothing that feels right about what just happened. Penny takes the cake, awkwardly smiles, and says, "Thanks."

Avarice looks at Lust and says, "Can I have a bite?"

Lust says, "Of course, oh yes definitely. I love tempting people." She offers him a bite, holding out her fork.

Wrath wedges himself between Lust and Penny. He opens his mouth and says, "Hey, hey, how about right here?"

Lust says in a baby doll voice, "Oh I'm sorry. Of course, here you go."

Envy, who is seated across the table, looks at all this, looks at Lust, and says, "I want some, too. Don't forget about me."

Lust looks down at an empty plate and says, "Oh no, I'm out." She looks over at Avarice and with a playful smile says, "Will you go get me some more?"

He looks back and says, "Of course."

He brings the new piece of cake to Lust, who gives a bite to Envy.

Lust offers a bite to Sloth. He says, "No, couldn't be bothered to get up and walk to the other side of the table."

Looking over toward Gluttony, Lust asks, but already knows the answer, "I'm guessing you don't need a bite of my slice of chocolate cake."

"Always room for more." He, in one quick gulp, devours the bite of cake off Lust's fork. Gluttony returns his attention to the entire chocolate cake in front of him and is digging his fork in for another bite.

No one offered Despair any cake.

Penny asks Despair, "How are you doing with the lectures?"

Despair looks at Penny, thankful for acknowledgment or even a kind word, and says "Ok, I guess. I am having a little trouble with..."

Wrath interrupts Despair, "Penny, did the change up with Gluttony and Avarice throw you off?"

"I am always prepared. Change is inevitable. I know the material. I know it well enough that when one of you isn't prepared, I will be able to deliver. Do you honestly think I am stupid enough to rely on any of you?" Penny says with a confident air.

THE DEVIL MOTIONS TO Penny to come closer to him. She gets up and walks over to him in the cafeteria.

"I just wanted to congratulate you or at least thank you for noticing and talking to Despair. I think she is having a tough time. I know how busy you are with preparing for the lead soul catcher competition and I just wanted to let you know I am not unaware that you are taking into account other demons. Let's face it that lead soul catcher position requires someone to keep close tabs on everyone and be able to assist or at least be aware when there might be a concern. Managerial roles are not for everyone."

"Thank you, sir," Penny says.

"Well, I don't want to keep you. I will let you get back to the other demons."

Penny nods. She starts to walk back to the table, sees the angel, and immediately says, "Alright, who are you and why in the world are you constantly following me? I thought for certain you were Avarice, but clearly you are not. I thought you were Wrath, but he's denying it. So who are you? Why are you here? And why are you bothering me?"

The angel looks at Penny and says, "Ok, first calm down. You should know, right now, I'm inside your mind, so no one can see me, but you. This means you're having a very vivid conversation with no one, like you're wildly flailing your arms. I'm enjoying all the emotions that you're having, but no one can see me. They just see you wildly talking to yourself. I was just coming by to say 'hi'. I didn't want to be rude and I didn't always want to be coming into your dorm. So I thought I'd say hi in the cafeteria. You know, where we've met before. It's like a little reunion. I can see your upset. I'll leave," with that the angel leaves.

Penny shakes her head and looks down. She sees the devil's shoes, looks up, and says, "Are you actually standing here or are you in my head, too?"

The devil very concerned says, "No dear, I'm standing here in front of you. You seem to be having a very animated conversation all by yourself. So I thought maybe I should check on you. So, what's going on?"

"That angel keeps coming back. She keeps getting into my head. Is this something, that's happening to other demons or is this just a special treat for me?" Penny asks.

"No, it's kind of just a special treat for you right now. Don't worry, when you get back to your non-mortal form, I can show you how to block her, so she's not in your thoughts. For right now, I have to keep you in mortal form. So you're going to be subject to all these little invasions."

He then looks at Penny and thinks 'Well, I guess the angels must think highly of you and must want you. That's interesting, and bad for me.'

Penny looks at the devil and says, "I am the embodiment of pride. I am a demon and I've worked very hard to represent pride. I know who I am; I know what I want; and I'm not getting sidetracked now. I've put in too much time and effort to become exactly and precisely who I am. How do I get this to stop?

"I just want to prepare and explain the sin of pride, which shouldn't even be considered a sin. My recognition of my hard work should not be a sin. It's just me doing what I'm supposed to do and I happen to be doing it better than everybody else."

The devil smiles, looks at her, and says, "Don't worry dear. All this is telling me, is that you are quite ready to be lead soul catcher, should the job be offered to you. Now let's have you scamper off to the library. Don't worry, pride is my favorite sin, it's what I'm most known for. So worry not, this being, this angel, who keeps getting into your thoughts has bitten off a little more than she can chew. It's probably some beginner angel, who thought, 'oh I'm going to try to get into Penny's head.' Very soon you'll be back to all your full powers. I'll show you how to block the being and none of this will matter."

With that Penny relaxes and thinks 'ok, all is going to return to normal and even the devil thinks I would make a good lead soul catcher. All is right, all is well.'

Penny smiles, leaves, and walks toward the library. She stops in her tracks and thinks to herself *the devil just admitted there is an angel and she is trying to get me. That's interesting!*

———

Penny is in the library setting up all her books and her notes. She looks down at a blank notebook. She knows how to do all of this. She knows how to research; be alone; read a book; and write down her notes. She is not connected to anyone right now. She is in her element. It is all her. It's all Penny; no one but Penny.

She begins writing out her notes for the sin of avarice. Ok this is interesting. It's not always about wanting more. It's more, you're thinking about yourself and how others can give you what you want without you considering what others want or need. As in, you don't see or consider your fellow man.

Penny is getting involved into her studies. She feels a bit of calm over everything and then she looks up across the table and staring at her is the angel.

The angel says, "Hi, I think we kind of got off to a bad start. I don't want you to hate me. I admire you. We all admire you. We think you're doing a great job and I'm not trying to start anything."

Penny looks at her very angrily and says, "Ok first, are you actually here or am I once again talking vividly to myself."

The angel looks at Penny and says, "No, this time other people can see me. So you don't have that insane rant and rave thing going on. That was a lot to spring on you."

Penny says, "Ok what is the whole point? What's the point of you being here? Do you have an end game or are you just here to throw me off my game?"

The angel says, "Oh, I just want to let you know, we're always here. In case, well I don't know, in case you want to say hi or just know somebody's in your corner. We're here, Penny."

"You're in my corner, great! I'm a demon. I don't really need an angel in my corner. Seems weird, but ok thanks for letting me know, I'm not alone," Penny responds with a sarcastic head tilt and eye roll.

Penny thinks about it and says, "Even though being alone is exactly and precisely what I want to be. I want to study all the things I need to study for this exam coming up. The devil seems to think I am doing a great job."

Penny continues, "Is that the whole deal? Is it that you want to make sure I do or do not become the lead soul catcher? Do you have any goals or are you just chilling down here? Are you Lust? Oh, maybe you are Lust. She's good at temptation, that's kind of her thing. Maybe that's it, you're just here to tempt me so I don't study. Oh that is devious. I have to admit, I didn't see that one coming. I have to give you credit, Lust, you totally through me. Its good to know that I have to keep my guard up, that I can be thrown off by just a mere temptation."

The angel looks at Penny and says, "I'm not Lust. I wasn't sent here by Lust or by anyone. I just wanted to let you know we're always here and we're happy to help and all of that good stuff. I'm not anybody you know," with that, the angel disappears.

Penny sits thinking *Great now I'm all flustered. How am I supposed to get back to my studies.*

——

Outside the library, the devil is in the middle of yelling up to the sky and says, "Ok, I didn't think you were going to come down and suddenly mess with one of my demons. I like Penny. As you know, pride holds a special place in my heart. Why are you bothering with my pride? Why are you bothering Penny, my pride, with an angel. It's not like you're getting her back. She's mine. I get to keep her. You can't have her. Oh, this is a little game. We're going to see if we can take a demon from the devil. You're not taking any demons from the devil, most certainly not Penny. She's mine. Don't go messing with Penny."

The angel appears. She calmly says, "You wanted to make some of your demons mortal for a short time. You did this with hopes of enticing more people to go to Hell. God allowed you to make a few demons mortal for a short time. Mortals have the free will to believe in salvation. If a mortal dies, and you wanted your demons to be mortal, then they are judged and potentially saved. You may have done this so your demons get better at tempting mortals, but it sounds to me like the mortal demons are fair game."

The devil looks at the angel. He is scared and the angel knows it.

"You risked your demons to lure more people into Hell. I just noticed a loophole. I didn't create the loophole, I am just taking advantage of it," with that the angel leaves.

VICTORIA W THOMSON

Greetings reader: I am not happy. I am not happy, at all.

Chapter 8 Gluttony

"NOW WE CAN TALK ABOUT one of the most versatile sins we have. Let me say there is nothing yummier, but I'll let Gluttony do all the explaining. Gluttony, could you come down and explain all this." The devil motions for this ordinary looking demon in a blue oxford shirt and khaki pants to come to the front of the lecture hall.

"I know, I'm not the morbidly obese person you were expecting, but don't worry, I'll explain."

"As you can see, sometimes I'm really fat; and sometimes I'm really skinny; and sometimes I'm really picky. I am also sometimes drunk. You're thinking how is that gluttony. I'll explain, it's really more of a preoccupation with something. The preoccupation is such that, you are so preoccupied with whatever it is you are being gluttonous about, that you fail to notice God; or your fellow man; or really give a crap about anything else

"Usually this falls into one of several categories. The first one is obvious. Let me eat and eat and you're eating food and you're not noticing you're doing it to excess or doing it to not deal with things. You're doing it while other people are without food. You're not taking into account your fellow man.

"God wants you to eat. God wants you to have that piece of cake; that's not the problem. The problem is when you get too big a piece of cake. You have that first bite and you're like this is yummy. By the time you get three-quarters through the piece, you're like 'Will this piece of cake ever end?' Despite the feeling changing from positive to negative, you keep eating the cake.

"Or you have a big bag of Doritos and you eat the whole bag and at the end, you not only didn't even enjoy eating the last half, you don't even remember eating the last half. God wants you to remember and enjoy food.

"You're mindlessly eating, works out wonderfully for me. Mindlessly doing something, mindlessly consuming more than you were expecting to is a way to separate you from Christ and if you do that, then I get a chance to get your soul.

"Another way that gluttony is in charge, that no one thinks about is anorexia. They're preoccupied with food. In that case, it is not a failing on their part, it's a disease. It's a disease of the mind, which means I'm involved. I'm just not telling anyone, I'm involved. The anorexic is preoccupied with food, to the point that the people who love the anorexic are worried sick about them. Despite this, the anorexic can't change their preoccupation with food. There's nothing they can do because I'm in charge.

"The third group of people are particularly picky. I can usually get young kids to do this. It doesn't work for very long. It's just kind of fun for me.

"Little kids say 'I only want my chicken nuggets on the blue plate. I only want there to be three of them, exactly three. They have to be at least two inches from the potatoes. If they're touching the potatoes, I'm not eating tonight.' That kind of nonsense usually doesn't get to continue. It doesn't really matter. It just lets me get to know the toddler, so when they see me later, we've already met.

"There is also eating in the wrong place or wrong time.

"There is also using food as judgement. For example, not considering your fellow man. Say you're a vegan, not one of the quiet vegans, you're one of the vegans, who thinks they're better than everyone. If you're one of these people, trust me, I'll be there. I probably want to watch as you judge every other person."

Gluttony stops for a minute, he turns looks at the devil, and says, "I have no idea how to explain this. It seems, like it wouldn't be a problem for anyone to understand, if I could keep it simple. Look if you're fat, you're not a bad person. Everybody wants that nice easy answer, but it's not like that.

"It's not just you're fat; so you're a bad person. It's not a case of, oh you let yourself enjoy this one item. It's that you allowed food, or an obsession, to come between you and other people. You made food or whatever it is that you're consuming come between you and Christ.

"It is the reason ...," with that Gluttony looks at the class, his brow furrows, and says, "This is not working. Sorry, I don't know what's wrong with me, but I just can't..."

With that he left the room, all of the demons turn looking around, until Avarice says, "What was up with that?"

The devil moves to the front of the room and says, "Ok, even I don't know what to do with that, but I'll deal with whatever that was, later."

The devil looks over at Penny and says, "Well my dear, you always know the right thing to say. You're always prepared, ready for anything, and everything. Why don't you come down and dazzle us with your brilliance and more importantly, save me."

Penny walks to the front of the room and says "Well, I do have an outline available of various things that count as gluttonous behavior and we can use that to take various souls."

The other demons roll their eyes at Penny's preparedness. She doesn't care. She is just happy to be ready and to show that she is ready. Penny finishes explaining the sin of gluttony.

At the end of class the devil says, "I knew you'd be prepared. You are always prepared."

Penny smiles, she enjoys getting the attention and the praise. She knows she got the praise and attention because she did the work, last night, just in case, she got ready to recite the main points. She got ready to teach the class. She did not go out with the other demons, so that if she was called upon; she could explain everything.

She takes great pride in always being ready and there's nothing wrong with pride, but when she was done and leaving the lecture hall, she continued to think about what a good job she had done. She did not immediately go and find the demon, Gluttony, and find out why he was upset. She isn't thinking of a fellow mortal, even a temporary demon mortal. At least not right away.

Eventually, Penny walks down to the cafeteria and finds Gluttony. "Hey, how you doing?"

Gluttony responds, "You are the only demon who has come to check on me. I don't know what happened to me. I guess I'm just not crazy about being up in front of people. My sin avoids a lot of deep introspection."

"Ok, but I've seen you yell at a lot of people, like I've seen you make some of them cry."

"Yes, but in those cases, it's a one-on-one situation. They are cases where I am in control. When it's me standing in front of a room full of demons, all staring at me, it's just a little too much."

Penny nods. She wants to understand, but she has no problem speaking in front of a large group, so she really couldn't understand.

———

Greetings again reader, you are coming upon one of the most important demons, Fallon. He does a great deal for me. You could say he lives for me or you could say he lives because of me. Either way. I give you chapter 9.

Chapter 9 Fallon

Several regular mortal college students notice the devil going into room 13 – 18. One of the students comments, "That's a weird room number. Where does it go?"

The devil answers, "I'm just an adjunct professor here. So, this leads to my office way down in Hell."

The students chuckle and one says, "Well, at least you got an office."

"It was a revelation to me."

The devil smiles at them as they walk away. He opens the door, which leads directly to his office in Hell. He takes a seat behind the mahogany desk in his office. There is a second door, on the other side of his office, that leads to Schomolance Academy in Hell. This second door opens and in walks Fallon. He is a demon and essentially the devil's assistant. He's holding a glass of bourbon.

"I see you're back from Earth. Did everything go well?"

"Yes, Earth gets a little too intense, sometimes. I just needed to take a break, get back to where everything is familiar and makes sense. The situation is getting sticky. I have this angel, who came out of nowhere, and now thinks she can outfox me. She found a loophole and is trying to utilize it against me."

Fallon hands the devil his drink and says, "Obviously, she's going to need to learn who she is dealing with. Still, an unfortunate mess for you to deal with, sir."

The devil looks at Fallon, gives a smile about the drink, and says, "How do you always know to do this?"

"How do I know to do what, Sir?"

"Always have a drink ready for me?"

"It is the reason I exist, literally. I am here to serve you. I need to have the drink ready, before you ask for it. As for this angel, I think you're correct. She is a young upstart. She will soon learn who she's dealing with and it will likely require her learning a lesson."

Fallon continues, "How do things look regarding the demons and the lead soul catcher position?" Fallon asks, as he straightens up the papers on the desk.

"On that front, at least, it's good. Lust is doing a good job. She understands temptation. She was made for it. She understands how to utilize it, and she doesn't particularly care about anybody. So, that's exactly right for her.

"Avarice was impressive in his lecture. He not only knew his stuff, he knew to work with the demons in R&D. Together they came up with some truly amazing things. I see great potential there. He should be great, this not being his first time around.

"Pride is doing phenomenally well. She's a young demon, but impressive. She's working hard, as pride usually does. Penny, this version of pride, likes to be called Penny. It's rather a sticking point with her. At any rate, Penny is the one being targeted by the angel," the devil says.

He continues, "I'm going to have to act a little differently around this demon. I think give her the mentor father figure version of the devil. She's mortal right now so she only sees what she wants to see and hears what she wants to hear. This resulted in me actually having to say skedaddle or at least her hearing skedaddle. Can you imagine me saying skedaddle?"

Fallon chuckles and shakes his head, before saying, "No, I can't. I'm sure it was fun though. You always know the right thing to say for each person. I'm sure you're adequately sizing up what she needs and saying what she needs to hear."

"The angel saw the weakness of a young demon and figured that was her easiest in?" Fallon asks, almost confirms.

"Probably, but it still makes a mess that I have to deal with or at least, keep an eye on," answers the devil.

"So, Avarice is currently in the lead for lead soul catcher," says Fallon.

"Gluttony gave his speech, but couldn't finish and just left the room."

"Oh dear, why?"

"You know, I forgot to follow up and ask." The devil chuckles. "Oh well, it's not like I care why. It just makes my job of selecting a lead soul catcher easier."

"I've only heard Lust, Avarice, and Gluttony give their presentations. Lust is technically the embodiment of lust. I don't think she will be the lead soul catcher. I just don't feel it. Felt her though, that was nice. Avarice impressed me more. Obviously, Gluttony is out. Pride/Penny, I think will impress me, when we get to her speech. Next is Envy; I do not have high hopes."

"Well there is always Despair," Fallon says. The devil and Fallon look at each other and just start to laugh.

"Oh Fallon, thank you. I needed a laugh after all that I have been through," says the devil.

"And now I have to get back to Earth. I don't want to, but I can't hide in Hell forever, even if I would desperately like to." The devil walks out the office door that leads back to the college.

Chapter 10 Sloth

E nvy scans the lecture hall looking for Lust. Immediately, she moves toward Lust and says, "I want you to do something for me."

Lust looks at her and says, "Ooh are your mortal desires getting to you? I'd be happy to help."

Envy says, "No, I want something else."

Lust looks at her and says, "What do you want?"

"I want you to go to Sloth and convince him to give his speech today, instead of tomorrow."

"Why would I want to do that?" Lust asks.

Envy answers, "You want to do that because he will not be prepared to deliver his speech today. You want to be lead soul catcher. He will look incompetent knocking him out of the running, which helps you. As for me, I get what I want, which is to not deliver my speech today. Lets face it, you're the best person for getting a man to do what you want." Lust smiles at the compliment. Envy smiles knowing she just got Lust to behave exactly as she wanted.

Lust thinks about it and says, "Ok, although, I was never really worried about Sloth, but let's just go ahead and lessen the competition."

HE WHO DOES NOT EXIST

Lust slinks up to Sloth and smiles at him. He looked at her with a look of excitement and desire on his face, like he almost has interest in something. She purrs into his ear, "Hi Sloth, I was wondering, are we going to get to hear your speech today?"

He says, "No, it's Envy's turn."

"But Sloth, I really want to hear your speech today. Could you possibly deliver your speech today? I really wanna hear it."

Suddenly all he wanted to do was give her what she wanted. He answers, "Yeah, I-I can do that. I can give you what you want."

Lust looks at Sloth and says, "Thank you so much." She, then, gives him a little kiss and walks away.

The devil overhears this and says, "What's all this now? We're changing around my syllabus, again? Does no one care about what I want? Is this not my classroom anymore, hmm? When did I lose complete and utter control?"

Envy looks at the devil and says, "Sloth wants to give his speech today."

The devil looks at Envy and says, "Oh Sloth does, does he? In other words, you don't want to do your speech, so you're having Sloth do his speech, instead. You used Lust to make Sloth do what you want. Is that what's going on?"

Envy looks at the devil and says, "I want to go on a different day. I don't want to go today."

The devil looks at Sloth and says, "Are you willing to go today?"

Sloth says, "Yeah, I don't care."

The devil turns looks at Envy and says, "Let me be clear. I want you to deliver your speech tomorrow. No excuses. This is what I want."

Envy looks at the devil and says, "If it's what you want."

The devil looks at her and says, "It is what I want."

Envy looks at the devil and says, "Well the devil gets, what the devil wants."

The devil looks at Envy and realizes he has just been a pawn in her game. He doesn't know whether he is impressed or annoyed.

Everybody takes their seats. Penny leans over to Lust and says, "What was all that about?"

Lust says, "I don't know. Envy didn't want to go today. So we're hearing Sloth and apparently, I was used."

"Oh great. I prepared for Envy's speech. I'm only moderately prepared for Sloth's speech, but whatever, it's not like Sloth is gonna knock it out of the park. Still, I would have liked to have been ready to take over for him."

Sloth walks to the front of the lecture hall and stands in front of the table with the lectern on it. He is shabbily dressed in jeans and an untucked t-shirt. He takes a deep breath, looks at the class, and says, "Ok, apparently, I'm doing my speech today. It was supposed to be tomorrow, but people wanted me to move it. You should know that a long time ago I was two sins. I used to be acedia and tristitia. Easiest way to remember this is acedia is like apathy; tristitia is like being super sad, also known as, despair. Come to think of it, Despair why don't you come down here for a minute."

Despair walks to the front of the room, sheepishly looks at the class, and gives a little wave and says, "Hi."

Sloth continues, "For some reason, we were combined. It's not like I care, but now, we've been separated and I have a new name. You have no idea how much I would rather have Despair stay down here and give her speech, instead of me giving my speech."

The devil, then, yells, "No, you students have messed with my syllabus enough. Sloth you are giving your speech today. Envy, YOU will give your speech tomorrow. Enough with these games." Despair returns to her seat.

Sloth says, "Right, sorry about all that. As I'm sure you've heard, Lust used me because Envy used her and that's why you're hearing me speak today and not Envy. I know you're thinking the same thing everyone else is; how am I even a deadly sin.

"I mean I'm not deadly, I'm laid back. Everybody knows that. I'm also known as procrastination. I'm a quiet sin. I'm why people just don't get things done. They let poverty and hunger continue in the world. They couldn't be bothered with their fellow man. So, that's why hunger and poverty still exist in the world.

"I let apathy take over. I let the 'I don't care' or 'I'll get to it tomorrow' take over. People numb themselves with TV, computers, or a million other things. Anything so they don't have to think about the problem at hand. They now have the expression 'that is future me's problem.' They just hope it will work itself out.

"Here's the danger, it works itself out so that some people have a lot of money, and some people are starving. Some people have to survive on less than a dollar a day. Actually, the mortals just rejoiced because instead of it being less than a dollar a day, they got it to $2.00 a day. Yep, I got things so bad that people are living on less than $2.00 a day.

"You need to adjust your thinking about sloth. I was close to giving this big long speech, but why. I just prevent people from putting any effort into making things better for one another.

"I make it so they do not accomplish anything. I do this quietly. I don't need, nor care for the fanfare. And if you take a look at the Earth, particularly this country, I'm doing a good job. Everyone is just exhausted. The best meme I read 'All I do is work and sleep and yet I have no money and I'm exhausted.'

"That's sloth. So I get it, none of you think I'm deadly. I'm fine with that. I'm fine with that because, like the devil, none of you think I exist. None of you think I'm a problem, but in reality, I have very quietly, like a virus, taken over. I make it so you don't accomplish a lot of things and you're ok with it. I haven't gotten to everyone, but I've gotten the masses. The majority of people may be outraged, but they're not constructively doing anything about it.

"So I'm very quietly destroying the world and even better, no one cares that I'm doing it or is even worried about stopping me from doing it. I don't think I have much more to say on the subject. I'm just quietly destroying the Earth, but that seems to be what you want. Isn't it?"

The devil puts his hand to his head and says, "Wow, you truly have mastered the art of not being noticed. I will tell you, I have not given you any regard or consideration as an actual contender, but wow, you are a contender. Your results are truly amazing. I'm just sort of floored at the moment.

"All right class while I digest this I guess we're getting out early today so I'll see you tomorrow."

HE WHO DOES NOT EXIST

Penny is getting up to leave class and Despair looks at her. Penny knows she wants to say something. Finally, Despair says, "I wonder if you'll come with me? I kind of want to go to the Chapel on campus."

"Ok," Penny answers. "Why do you want to go there? I'm happy to go with you, no problem, but what are we going to do there?"

Despair says, "I don't know. I just, I just kind of want to go and see what's there."

Penny says, "Ok then that's where we'll go."

Penny's thinking *Despair never reaches out to anyone. Never really talks to anyone, but ok, it's not a big ask. We can certainly walk over there and now that we're mortal we can go inside.*

At this point the devil looks at Penny quizzically and Penny answers his look back with a dumbfounded look 'of I don't know I'm just following Despair.' Penny and Despair leave the lecture hall together.

Chapter 11 The Chapel

Penny and Despair walk together toward the chapel. For now, they are mortal, they can go into a chapel with no problem. Once they are back to being demons, they aren't allowed in the chapel. Inside Despair looks at a picture of the crucifix on the wall and turns toward Penny.

"Do you think it hurt?" asks Despair.

Penny shrugs and looks at the crucifix and says, "Looks like it did."

Despair reads the words underneath the picture, "For God so loved the world, that he gave his only Son, that whoever believes in him should not perish but have eternal life."

Despair looks at Penny and says, "So he did this because he loved people?"

Penny answers, "I don't know, that's what the sign says."

Despair says, "I wish somebody loved me."

Penny replies, "We're demons. We don't get love."

Despair looks at Penny and says, "I know, I just wish someone loved me. I wish I knew what love was. I wish someone cared."

Penny says, "Yeah, well, I don't know what to tell you. It ain't gonna happen."

Despair kind of shrugs and they continue to look at all the pictures on the wall. It was a college campus chapel. It was trying to represent everyone. They had a few other religious pictures on the wall, but it was essentially a Christian chapel trying to be more. The newly mortal demons sit in one of the pews quietly and look down.

It is, on the one hand fun, because they know they aren't really supposed to be there or more of they never could be there because demons can't go into a chapel. On the other hand, it is a little sad, because they know, they would never feel this level of love and acceptance and happiness, again. They could feel the power of the chapel. They are a little saddened because for the first time, they know and understand that once they were back to being demons, they could never go in and feel this love again.

Penny takes a deep inhale and gives a deep exhale. Her heart rate lowers. Despair looks over at Penny and says, "I don't want to leave. I know, I have to leave. I understand I have classes and everything else, but I really like being in here. I don't want to leave."

Penny looks back at her and says "We have lectures to attend. We have lunch to eat. As much as, you want to stay here, we have things to do."

Despair replies "I don't care. I'm finally somewhere I don't feel horrible. It's like I had a heavy weight on my shoulders and for the first time that heavy weight isn't there."

Penny says, "Despair, that heavy weight is your coat. It's cold and sorry you have to put the coat back on. We gotta go back out there."

Penny looks at her watch and says, "We must go out there. I have to get to the library because there are speeches coming up and I need to be ready. Let's face it, no one's going to learn these sins for me. Then, I really need to feed this mortal body, again!" Penny's pulse quickens and her breathing shortens as she gathers her belongings. The two get up and leave the Chapel.

They walk down the Chapel stairs into the lawn a little bit and encounter the devil. "Ladies, what are we doing? Why are we coming out of the Chapel?" He is holding his wool overcoat close over his chest, up by his neck. He wants to look like he is cold, to blend in with everyone else.

"Well now that we're mortal, we actually get to go inside the chapel. It was kind of neat. It was like we got to go into the enemy's camp and look around."

The devil gives a half-hearted smile and says, "Just be careful. You are new to being mortal. I can't be having you die while you're up here. If you die, you really die and then I've gotta go replace you. That's a lot of paperwork on my part."

The devil looks beyond Penny and Despair. The angel, leaning against the chapel, gives him a little nod of acknowledgement. He gives her a nod of acknowledgement back.

"All right, well let me, let you get back to the cafeteria or whatever else it is you need to do. I have a few errands to run. I'll see you for Envy's lecture tomorrow, which better happen if she knows what's good for her," says the devil.

The two demons walk off toward the library and the devil walks towards the chapel. The angel comes down the chapel stairs and looks at the devil and says, "Sorry, you can't come in here. You know, you're the devil and all that."

The devil looks at her and says, "Yeah, I'm not trying to get into the chapel, but thanks. Why are you bothering my demons?"

"Your demons came to me. I didn't go to them. You know, now that they're not in Hell and they're mortal, they're welcome to come into the chapel. Let's face it, while they're on Earth and mortal, they're not under your protection, like they are in Schomolance Academy. You got a little exception for one lecture hall, otherwise, we're all up in some little New England College that nobody knows about. You can't protect them outside your classroom. They're fair game and they walked into the chapel. I didn't chase after them. They came to me freely," says the angel.

The devil looks at the angel a little angry and asks, "What is your problem? I've done this before, no concern whatsoever. You get involved and you want to take one of my demons. Why? Why isn't this going like it normally does?"

The angel looks at the devil and says, "Simple: your pride was getting a little too big. Your pride. I am not talking about your little demon, Penny. I'm talking about your pride.

"You seem to think you have a right to come up here and tempt mortals, as much as you want. Basically, you forgot that God allows you to do this. You don't have a right to do this. There's a risk every time. You forgot about the risk. So, I'm here to remind you. They are mortal, they are on Earth, they are fair game.

"The risk you keep forgetting to calculate is going to cost you, a minimum, of one demon and I might go for a second demon.

"If I take Pride, you're going to care. You are all about your Pride, in this case your precious Penny. Let's face it. It is your favorite deadly sin, that's the one that got you kicked out of heaven, isn't it? Yeah, I might take your Pride, again. You know to remind you that God is in charge, not you."

The devil looks a little concerned and says to the angel, "What do you mean you're gonna try to take my pride, I mean Penny? She's my pride. Don't take my pride." He says, with a quiver in his voice, like he knew he had gone too far and there could be consequences.

The angel laughs and says, "Your pride might get in the way of your success, again"

The devil says, "Pride is my gateway sin. I get a lot of people into Hell with that sin. I'll have to train up a new demon to replace Penny. That'll set me back. It isn't fair."

The devil then quickly offers a bargain. "Ok, I can see how I have upset God. How about you take Despair and one of the demons from down in Schomolance Academy? Your pick, I have lots of demons down there."

The angel laughs. "I am not here to make deals. We think we got a chance at getting Penny. You knew the risks when you put the demons on Earth and made them mortal. You got all cocky thinking oh I don't have anything to worry about. I can do whatever I want, I'm the devil. Well that's not how this works. Both of us are equally matched. You put them on Earth. I get to try to lead them to Christ."

HE WHO DOES NOT EXIST

The devil looks at the angel directly and says, "I don't think I have anything to worry about, with that one. She is quite focused on her studies and on being the best. I do not think you will get her. The pride is strong with that one. I'll get to keep her that's, just how it is. I know all about Penny. I've been grooming her for a long time." The devil says trying to sound confident.

The angel kind of shrugs and says, "We'll see."

The devil goes off in search of Penny to make sure she's doing what he expects.

———

Penny was, of course, studying in the library. She is ensuring she knows each sin well enough that she could give the lecture. All her, she is preparing as if it will be all her.

The devil gives a sigh of relief, Penny is exactly where he expected her to be.

"My darling, Penny, how are you? Are we doing good, studying hard?"

Penny looks up from her books, smiles, and says, "Yes, getting a handle on everything Avarice said."

A voice comes from in between the rows of books and says, "It all comes down to comparison. They want to look better than their neighbors, so they buy more. Classic envy problem. I must thank him for describing my sin."

The devil and Penny look and it's Envy. She puts back a book, gives a little smile, and says to the devil "Yes, I'm gonna do my speech tomorrow, relax. Right now, I think I'm gonna go to lunch. Want to join me, Penny?"

The devil gets a big smile on his face and says "Excellent, I will leave you girls to get lunch." The devil is quite happy, everything seems to be returning to normal in his little endeavor regarding the demons, people are listening to him again; Penny is studying; no one is going into chapels; everything is as it should be.

———

Envy and Penny walk into the cafeteria, where they see the other demons eating. They order some lunch; walk over to the table; and sit down.

Lust says, "I am getting a little sick and tired of constantly having to feed this mortal body. Oh and if I'm not careful I get pudgy, what is this crap?"

Wrath takes the seat next to Lust, grabs her waist, and says, "Some of us like a little extra pudge."

Lust gives a little squeal and kisses Wrath.

Penny and Envy sit next to Lust and Wrath. The demons sit around the table in the order of Penny, Envy, Lust, Wrath, Avarice, Gluttony, Sloth, and an empty chair. Despair walks in and joins the group, sitting in the empty chair next to Sloth. She is happy to be part of the group of demons. The last time she felt she was a part of anything was when she and Sloth were one sin. She still feels the separation very deeply.

"Did Penny tell you where we went today?" says Despair. The demons looked quizzically at Penny and Despair.

Despair continues, "We went to the Chapel. It was wonderful. It was calm. It was acceptance. It was just a very deep feeling of everything is ok or is going to be ok. I don't know how to describe it. Kind of like someone is here to take away all the pain, or at least be with you and your pain, so you're not alone.

"All your concerns kind of melt away and apparently there's this guy who suffered very much because he loved people. It was nice to hear somebody loved us or at least the mortal us." Despair almost smiles as she finishes speaking.

The other demons look at Despair, kind of amazed that she is speaking. They are also a little taken aback that there exists such as space, as the chapel.

Penny says to the group, "Yeah, we went into the chapel. It was very nice. They had these big long pews for everyone to sit in. Various religious images were on the wall. It was definitely more of a Christian Chapel than anything else, but they at least paid homage to a few of the other religions. But, yeah we got to go into the enemy's camp, very fun to poke around. We ran into the devil as we were leaving. All in all it was a very interesting little side trip. I think I'd put it more that way." The demons nod at Penny.

"I wanna go back," Despair says quietly, so quietly, she doubts anyone hears.

Sloth hears Despair. He feels the separation as well. Penny hears and looks at Despair and says "Ok. Well, maybe on another day."

Penny then thinks she sees the angel, but decides to keep her attention with the group.

Chapter 12 Envy

Everyone is back in the lecture hall. "What excuse are you going to use today, Envy?" asks Avarice, laughing with Wrath and Gluttony.

"You can forget about conning me to go today," chimed in Wrath.

She gives the other demons a serious look, as she walks to the front of the room, before the devil even calls her name.

"I am about more than want. I am about comparison. I just want to be better than you. Actually that's not entirely true. Well first let me separate me as a demon, from what my sin does. I'm incredibly intelligent and incredibly manipulative. I will make you feel whatever I need to make you feel to control the situation and to control you. When I have targeted the mortal I want, their happiness is gone. All that matters is my getting their soul.

"How this works is my mark, I mean my mortal, wants to be better than the person in question. They usually don't want to work for it because let's face it, if you work for something, you might fail and also that's a lot of effort.

"This is just one of the reasons why, I am the opposite of pride. Pride will see something that she wants; make a plan; and start working the plan, until she achieves what she wants.

The last thing in the world pride wants is to make the other person give her less than a good fair competition. Pride wants to genuinely earn being better. That's lovely. That's not how I work.

"Here is how I work. I will literally destroy the other person, if I think that's what's necessary for me to win. I will injure the competition, no problem. I win at all costs. I don't need to fight fair. When I get a hold of a mortal, they don't care whether they truly win or not. They care whether they get the crown, the medal, the promotion, or whatever.

"I make mortals care so much about others not winning, that let's say someone pours their heart and soul into doing something, my mortal is that little internet troll in the background. They tear their competition down. My mortal knows they're not going to put in the time, effort, and energy to do something with their life or create something. Why should the competition get glory? I mean that's not fair to me. No no no! I get the glory not you.

"Ok, I am somewhat my own sin, except I don't just want to destroy the competition, I want to damn my mortal, too. My sin is the only currently recognized sin." Envy glares at Despair before continuing, "That has no happiness component. I mean Lust lets you enjoy sex in the short term. With Avarice, you enjoy the accumulation. While you are indulging, Gluttony has pleasure. Wrath enjoys the fight. Envy is a sin without pleasure. Once I grab hold of a mortal, I slowly turn them into a shell of who they once were.

"Let me tell you about my latest escapade. The devil and Penny both saw me in the library yesterday. I let them think I was preparing for this speech so that I'd look like a good student. I do care about that lead soul catcher position, but I care about it in my own special way. I will tear the rest of you down to get it and that's how this sin works. I'm not gonna waste my days in the library, studying really hard, and giving lots of good examples of envy over the years. Although my favorite quotation is by Gore Vidal. 'It is not enough merely to win; others must lose.'

"Here is how yesterday went. I saw the devil walk into the library; I slipped in right after him; and ran up to the section where he was. I overheard part of he and Penny's conversation and then at a time when I could be in the most control of the situation, I came out and said "Hi." Then, I invited Penny to lunch. The reason I invited Penny to lunch was because it stopped her from studying. Remember, I'm all about stopping someone else from succeeding. I really don't care if she succeeds or if she does a good job or that she gives me a good competition. She cares about all these things very deeply, but I don't. I want the success and I will tear someone else down to get it.

"My sin is about getting hold of a mortal and making that mortal believe someone else is the reason why they are not number one. If it weren't for this other person, they'd be recognized as the best. Of course, their focusing on the other person may be why they're not preparing, but that's not my concern.

"I get in and start to poison the soul of my target. I guess, in a way, that's what my sin represents. I am poison. Slowly I take over the mortal, until that mortal is filled with hatred.

"Everybody confuses me with jealousy. I don't care how I get in, once I'm in, I'm not leaving. Let me give you the difference. We've all heard the line, "I am a jealous God." Here's the deal, jealous is you're being protective. You already have what I want. Jealousy is 'hey don't take my boyfriend." Envy is I want your boyfriend. It is not, I want a boyfriend, who is like yours. I want that specific one. I begin to do whatever is necessary to get that boyfriend, or at least make sure the other mortal doesn't keep him. I will make my mortal do this to the point, they won't even notice there is another boy trying to win their love and affection. Why should anyone have a good relationship, I don't.

"Oh dear, this is not turning into a good speech at all. The devil wouldn't let me wait any longer. You see the reason I didn't want to give my speech earlier, was for comparison purposes. It's not that I have to be better than the seven of you. All I have to do is make sure the seven of you perform worse than me."

The devil just sits, blinking at Envy. After a very long pause, he finally says, "Ok Envy, that certainly was an enlightening speech. I have no idea what to say after that. Very diabolical, I'm quite happy.

"Class, I think I will leave it here today. You're dismissed."

The devil looks over at Despair and immediately projects himself into her mind and says, *Oh dear don't worry, no one's envious of you. I know you're envious of everyone though. That's not your fault, though. You were created to dwell, to over-think. Don't worry dear, you'll never be good enough." Despair's eyes kind of look down.*

Despair asks almost pleads with Penny to go to the chapel. The devil looks at Penny with a horrified angry look. Penny looks back and shrugs.

VICTORIA W THOMSON

She tells Despair, "Sure."
The devil storms out of the room.

Chapter 13 Fallon Two

The devil storms through his office college door marked 13 – 18; he is in his office in Schomolance Academy in Hell and yells, "Fallon!" No sooner had the words left his mouth, then Fallon is standing next to him with a double shot of bourbon.

"I can't believe she is doing this to me. Doesn't she know who I am? And while we're at it, why are my demons playing around in a chapel," says the devil, as he paces back and forth.

Fallon, with his usual calm demeanor and comforting smile upon his face says, "Master, why don't you tell me one thing, we will focus on that one thing, and then we'll focus on the next thing. I don't have your ability to listen to or pay attention to several things at once. I'm afraid I'm going to need you to slow down for me. I want nothing more than to help you. If you don't mind, why don't you start with telling me about the demons. How is the selection of lead soul catcher going?"

The devil takes a deep breath, looks at Fallon, and says "You're right. I need to look at this one thing at a time." He takes a deep breath and begins the run down.

"First, how the demons are doing. As I said earlier, Lust, while certainly adequate, very enjoyable to watch and what have you, she just doesn't have the managerial skills required.

There's still a bit of only looking out for herself. This is wonderful for a demon, but not so much for a manager of other demons.

"Next we have Avarice. Avarice gave a fantastic speech, fantastic examples of what he has done, and what he can do. He knew how to work with the demons down in research and development. He knew how to get mortals on a couple of levels. He knew what was involved. There was a certain finesse, a certain panache. He is definitely on the short list for lead soul catcher.

"Gluttony is out of the running. He is so caught up in his own mind, that he can't help himself, much less me. Thankfully that sin is easy to acquire and hard to get out of."

Fallon nods. He is trying to straighten up the devil's office while giving the devil his undivided attention, which of course was divided.

L"That brings us to Sloth. He was so much better at getting souls then I gave him credit for. I did not realize how much not caring mattered. Having people sit quietly on the sidelines and not getting involved. I didn't realize how dangerous and how horrible that really is or the problems it can cause. It not only causes a problem for them; they don't give a damn when their fellow man is harmed. It's really a lot more of a sin than I had ever given it credit for or given Sloth credit for. It's nice to know I can still be impressed. Humans never cease to amaze me. I was happy with how well Sloth did, as well. So he was surprising.

"Really don't know that I want to leave Sloth in charge and I know that he doesn't want to be in charge. Totally happy with the job he's doing, I'm just not sure he's looking for more responsibility.

"At any rate that gets us to Envy. She is downright maniacal. I mean she was so crafty, so impressive, and so destructive as a sin, that I got wrapped up in it. I mean she manipulated me, that's impressive."

Fallon stops straightening papers and looks at the devil wide eye upon hearing that the devil got wrapped up in Envy's presentation. The devil smiles and nods in return as if to say *yeah I couldn't believe it either.*

"I'm a little scared to be working that closely with her, but how she fooled me, the devil, that's really good and really deserves to be noticed. I'm not entirely sure I can trust her, which is problematic considering lead soul catcher is an elevated position, but you can't argue with her skill and intensity. She's definitely a top contender. Although, I have reservations. I'm not sure I can trust her, that's not necessarily a bad thing when you're evaluating a demon, but I'm not sure.

"On to nightmare number two, which might be linked with number three. Anyway this stupid angel just won't leave me alone. I have been up on Earth several times before. I got permission to make a few of my demons mortal. I mean doesn't God want his precious mortals to prove their faith and belief?

"All I want to do is make a few of my demons mortal for a short time. We come up to Earth, we get better at harvesting souls, and make it more of a fair fight, for us. Midway through, this angel comes down and says that I'm overstepping my bounds or that I'm doing too much.

"Now, I am supposedly not respecting God." Fallon scoffs in disbelief.

"Anyway, she's coming after my demons. I tried to offer her Despair. Let's face it, Despair never finishes anyway. I mean I don't know how many times we've done this whole bringing demons up to Earth, but Despair never makes it.

"We go through this every time we need to promote a demon to lead soul catcher. I know every time I do this, I put my demons at risk of being sent to Hell and being tortured. But really, I only lose Despair and she isn't even a separate deadly sin anymore. I just bring her because its fun to torture her. It reminds me of the old times in the 6th century, when she was her own deadly sin.

"I have no qualms about losing Despair. This angel is threatening to take my pride. She is saying that I, personally, have too much pride.

"I know, I'm going to win. Yes of course, I know I'm going to win, that's not the issue at hand. She's now really going after my demons. It's not a case of Despair just doesn't make it. It is a case of someone actively hunting my demons. They are mine. This little angel can't just take them. And who is she? Well, I know she's not as good as me. I don't know why she just won't leave me and my demons alone. She's getting under my skin; it's bothering me. It's just bothering me.

"The third reason I am concerned is that Penny went into a chapel with Despair." Fallon looks up at the devil again with disbelief.

"Are you kidding me? Like I need my demons going into chapels. Yes, I know they can go into chapels while they're mortal. Yes, I knew the risk. I just never thought they would go in. I might lose my demons to Him." The devil points upward.

"I mean sure, I lose some because they die, but if they die, they go down to Hell. We torture them for eternity. I haven't lost anything. They did. They lost their position in Hell. They went from being the torturer to being the tortured.

"No big deal for me. Now, you're telling me I could lose a demon maybe even two - to Heaven? This is getting ridiculous and to go after my pride. Seriously? Watching Penny come out of that chapel," the devil shakes his head, while looking down. Fallon just gives the devil an understanding look.

"I can still see the angel leaning on the outside of the chapel, kind of laughing at me, telling me I can't go into the chapel. I'm aware I can't go in the chapel. So this is what's going on." The devil drinks his double shot of bourbon in one gulp.

Fallon looks at the devil, pauses to digest all that the devil has been through, and suggests, "Ok so at this point, you can pack up all your demons and go back to Hell. Let everything cool off. The angel will think 'oh good, I got him to go back. Everything is fine.' She feels her big sense of victory and we just come back another day. We try again, later. I mean let's face it, she's not always down here. This is the first time you saw her. Let's just take everybody back to Hell and we'll come back in like a week or two. She'll think she's had her little victory. Everything will be fine." Fallon is happy with his suggestion.

The devil enlarges himself angry and red and says "I am in charge. I determine what we are doing. I call the shots and I say we stay. I'm going to beat her head on. Try to take my demons and especially my pride. What are you kidding me? You can't have my Penny. I have been grooming this demon, since the beginning. I even let her keep her name. I raised her pride to the point of keeping her name and individuality, not even just being known as Pride. I love that point about her. So, no, I am not just taking my demons and going back to Hell and letting the dust settle. I'm leaving them in the game. Nobody's going back to Hell. At this point, I'm ready to keep Despair, just to prove a point. We are going to stay. Everyone is going to give their speech. This trip counts!" The devil then exhales.

Fallon looks at him with a mix of confidence and concern. "Now there's my devil. Stop letting this foolish upstart of an angel throw you and get back up there."

Chapter 14 Back to the Chapel

Despair leaves the classroom and hurries toward the chapel. It is all Penny can do to keep up with her. Finally Penny says to her, "What are you, a demon on a mission?"

Despair answers. "No, I'm a mortal on a mission. I need to get back to that chapel. I need to get the devil out of my head. This is not going to continue. I'm going to pray."

Penny, trying to keep up, says, "Do you even know how to pray?"

Despair answers "No, but I'll figure it out." She keeps walking quickly across the lawn until she arrives at the chapel.

Inside the chapel, the angel lays down copies of the Lord's prayer and the apostles creed. The angel puts the copies in a spot where Despair couldn't miss them. The angel hears Despair and Penny walk in. She quickly hides in the corner of the chapel.

In a hushed tone, Despair says to Penny, "I can't do this anymore. I can't know there is a better way and not try to take it. I can't live with the devil inside my head. It just hurts too much. I am a tortured torturer and I can't deal anymore. The way I look at this, I have a chance." With that, Despair looks down at the apostle's creed and then looks up at Penny. Her eyes widen. With new found hope, she says, "Look here, it says

Jesus went to Hell. If he went to Hell and he made it out; then there's hope. Someone, somewhere made it out. Why can't I?"

Penny looks at Despair and says, "Well, he is the son of God, that whole God from God. You are not part of the Holy Trinity. You're not God's son. You're not God's daughter. You're a demon. I'll grant you, we're mortal for right now. We can die, but you got a long road between dying here on Earth and ascending to Heaven. This is not a guarantee by any means and I'm pretty sure you gotta let God know that you're good to go or at least want to go. You don't know how to let God know that you want to be on his side now. You're getting into dangerous waters and I don't want to see you get hurt. You do realize while we're on Earth, we can die, and if you think you're tortured now; you ain't seen nothing yet. You're going to be a tortured soul. It's gonna be what you have now, but with no relief.

"You need to think long and hard because right now, you're the one, who technically does the torturing. Yes I know the devil puts himself in your thoughts and makes you feel bad. At least, now, you can have moments, where you're with the other demons. You can get a cup of coffee with us. Ok, Hell doesn't have coffee. I mean you get breaks from the devil. It's an unrelenting thing when you start being tortured. It doesn't leave you alone. Now do you get it?"

"I am never without him, even when he is not actively in my head, I know that he can be in there at any time, and I don't want that anymore. I am done. And by the way, on the same piece of paper as the apostles creed, on the back side, is the Lord's prayer and I'm thinking that's a pretty good place to start praying. So, I'm going to start there."

She begins to read out loud:

Our Father, Who art in heaven, hallowed be Thy name; Thy kingdom come; Thy will be done on Earth as it is in heaven. Give us this day our daily bread; and forgive us our trespasses as we forgive those who trespass against us; and lead us not into temptation, but deliver us from evil.

"That's what I want. I want to be delivered from evil. I'm thinking here's a way to get away from evil, so, I see my chance and I'm taking it."

Penny looks at her and says, "Yeah, I think you're going beyond what I'm ready to sign up for here. I'm going to go ahead and leave you in the chapel. I'm going to go back to the other demons in the cafeteria. I'm just not ready to follow you, where you're going. I'm just not ready. You're turning your back on a lot of things, and for what? You don't even know that demons can be saved, mortal or not. You don't even know if God has the power to make us saved. You don't even know if God wants to save us. I'm sorry. I-I'm gonna go back to the cafeteria now.

———

Penny sees the angel out of the corner of her eye and walks over toward her. "So, is this all you're doing? You wanted to get Despair? Did I just help you get this far? What does this say about me? Is it actually possible for a demon to be saved?"

The angel looks at Penny and says, "I can't tell you the answers to the question you want. I can't give you any guarantees. Faith is about not having a guarantee, but still agreeing to believe. If you don't believe, then, even if I show you proof; it really won't work. If you want all the benefits of faith;

you have to have faith. There's no way around that." The angel walks toward Despair.

Penny turns and walks out of the chapel. She begins walking and ends up running toward the cafeteria to find the other demons.

———

She enters the cafeteria and sees the other six demons sitting at a table having a conversation. She takes a seat with them. Penny is shaking and out of breath. All the other demons look at her.

Gluttony says, "Where have you been? You and Despair ran out of that room after Envy's speech. What's going on? What are you guys doing?"

Penny looks at them and says, "It's Despair."

Sloth looks concerned and everyone else looks at Penny.

She continues, "She seems to really feel, she can be saved, and wants to convert to Christianity. I guess, I don't know. She's in the chapel right now. It's like her escape. It's her thing. I've never seen her like this. It's just odd."

Envy says, "What are you gonna do? Because you know and we know, you're the one to beat, for lead soul catcher. We don't like that you know you are in the lead, but you are. I don't know why, but you are. Are you out of the running? Are you going Christian, too?"

Penny says, "I-I don't even know what's going on. All I know is Despair is acting weird, like I've never seen her act. Granted, I wasn't super close with her before, but she's really going off the deep end. I don't think she's taking into account what she's giving up. I know she was never going to make lead soul catcher, let's face it. Still, I don't think she realizes that if she's wrong, if she says 'oh I'm going to go get saved' and then doesn't get saved, she's gonna be a tortured soul. While she might not like that she is Despair and without hope, at the very least, even as a tortured torturer as she is now, there are breaks in the torture. There are times when the devil isn't in her mind. She thinks, she's going to go up to Heaven and not have to worry about any of this. Even worse, there's no guarantee. She could go through all this and just end up in Hell as a tortured soul, not as the torturer of the tortured soul. I don't think she knows what she's doing. I don't think she knows what she's getting into and I'm a little worried, we both just got in over our heads. I got out in time, but I'm not sure if she did. In fact, the angel is talking to her now."

The other demons look at Penny and then each other. Avarice says, "Excuse me, the angel?"

Penny shakes her head and says, "Yeah, I have been talking to an angel, pretty early on, in this soul catcher selection process. At first, I didn't say anything because, I didn't really believe it myself. Then, I didn't know how to explain it, without looking weird to you guys, or have you guys see it as my weak spot. I didn't know if it was a strength or a weakness, yet. So, I was trying to get as much information as I could, before I revealed it. I'm pretty sure things have gotten weird and I need to reveal it. So, I don't know what's going on, but yeah, I've been talking to an angel."

The group just looks at Penny, until Avarice says, "All right, so you got an in on the other side"

Penny says, "I wouldn't go that far."

Envy looks at her and says, "Well let's face it, all my cards are on the table. Since I had to give my little speech and apparently, you have an in with an angel. I just feel like this is suddenly not a fair fight. I'm not saying I fight fair. I'm saying that I want to make sure you don't have any stuff the rest of us don't have; or if you do have this advantage, I want in, or I want someone to take that into consideration. All in all, I'm not happy"

Sloth looks at Penny and says, "Do you think we should talk to Despair? I mean should I make sure she's ok or what do I do because I don't want to do much; I prefer not to do anything, but if I absolutely have to do something, then I guess I should do something. Do I have to do anything?"

"Ok, first it's nice to see you care about anything and given your emotional state right now, no, I don't think you can help right now. I don't know what to do," said Penny.

Chapter 15 Wrath

As Despair walks into the class room, the devil smiles at Despair and says, "That's a pretty sweater."

Despair smiles, walks toward Penny, and says, "It's working. I prayed for the devil to be nicer to me and it's working."

"You don't know if that's what's happening or if you just have on a nice sweater, which you do by the way, great sweater." Penny says back to Despair and takes a seat in the front of the near empty lecture hall.

The devil walks to the front of the room and says, "Wrath, you're up."

"Hey everybody, what's up?" This tall, well built, muscular guy in a letterman jacket is addressing the class. Penny and the other demons are admiring Wrath's look, he is wearing really nice fitting jeans and a polo shirt under his letterman's jacket. His confidence and look made the other demons want to be near him, either as a friend or a lover.

"All right, so as many of you know, I can get angry from time to time. Ok, I'm angry most of the time. Here's the deal, just don't get me angry. Don't wrong me and I won't get angry. You wrong me, you disrespect me, we're gonna have a problem.

"The sin of wrath is all about taking anger a little too far. In fact, my representing the wrath department is a good idea. Let's face it, I'm good at what I do. I might have a thing with being overly concerned on getting even or being unbelievably angry, but hey, I have my reasons. I'm ok as long as no one gets on my bad side, which is really not that hard. It's just once you tick me off, I'm not really interested in affording you sympathy.

"Think about it, you're walking down the street and someone walks into you; there should be an apology. If there's not an apology, that's disrespectful. It is wrong. You don't do that; so I don't allow that.

"Some other examples, which I'll just quickly highlight. I love revenge. Every dictator is a fantastic example for the sin of wrath. There's no part of me that's like, 'yeah just let it go, whatever.' Even if it hurts me more in the long run, I want to make sure you hurt.

"Like Envy said in her lecture 'That whole, it's not enough that I win, others must lose.' In my case, it's not others, it's just the one who wronged me."

Wrath looks over at the devil and says, "Can I bring in an example?"

The devil kind of smiles and answers. "Sure, I don't care what you do."

With that, Wrath brings in someone from Hell, who in life was an abusive spouse. "All right, let's look inside this guy's mind." The demons use the skills they learned in the first lecture, about going into the mortal mind so they know what the mortal is thinking.

It was filled with anger and revenge. The demons were able to see into the abusive spouse's mind, heart, and former soul. There were so many emotions, the demons felt claustrophobic and choked with anger. It was hard to breathe. With the entirety of this person's being, the person just wanted everyone to respect them. He just wanted everyone to know that he was in charge; that it was his power. Everyone was someone trying to take his power away.

It was consuming, not only the anger, he just didn't care about anybody else. He just cared about revenge.

Wrath speaks, "You are looking into what my sin can do. Sometimes, the mortal realizes the problem in time. If they do, they can save themselves. When they don't, I get their soul.

"It's ok to get angry for a reasonable amount of time. It's ok to want revenge for a reasonable amount of time. Ok, there is probably no reasonable amount of time, but I love it. When anger starts to get unreasonable, when it starts to get a little too long, that's when you might need to think about changing things." With a snap of his fingers, Wrath returns the mortal to Hell.

The devil looks over and says, "Well I'm impressed with your conjuring ability. Sorry to interrupt, especially someone who's not going to be happy to be interrupted. I'm only interrupting you because you did a good job and if I don't get this point out, I'm gonna miss a golden opportunity."

Wrath begrudgingly nodded.

The devil continues, "Anyway, there's not much room in a mortal's mind. Keep that in mind, when you're trying to tempt them. If you go into a full mind, don't put anything else in there. Maybe the occasional, hey look at his shoes, but be very careful of saying anything. You don't want to distract the mortal so bad, that they turn to prayer." With that the devil looked at Wrath, who was angry and says, "Oh, sorry dear, this is your show, go right ahead."

Wrath looks back at the devil. He knows who he was getting angry at, but he is unable to stop himself. "Yeah that's what I was saying, You know keep it short sweet to the point because this guy's brain is already kind of full. Basically when you get a wrath case, just call it over to my department. This is what we specialize in. This is what we do, not you."

Penny looks at Wrath and wasn't really scared, but kind of put off by his whole aura. She thinks to herself, well she thought it was just to herself, 'you're good looking, but I'm not sure I want to deal with every other part of your personality that goes with those good looks.'

With that, Wrath gets into Penny's head and very angrily says, "You got a problem with me, Penny?"

Penny, in shock from Wrath projecting himself into her mind, pushes back against her chair and quietly answers, "No."

The devil then pushes in and says, "Ok Wrath, down boy. Go back to the front of the room. Better yet, just, just go back to your seat."

Penny cowers. Wrath entering her mind felt like an invasion of privacy.

The devil speaks to Penny in a calm voice, almost a whisper, like he was the parent and she was the child. "My goodness, I'm not going to let someone hurt my Penny. You're safe Penny, don't worry. Are you okay? Are you scared?"

Penny looks at the devil and says, "No." She is still shaking.

"It seems like more is wrong, what's going on?" asks the devil looking concerned.

Penny confesses to the devil how she and Despair went back to the chapel and how it seems like Despair was getting really close to the angel. At this point the words were just coming out of Penny and she couldn't stop. She says to the devil, "Despair talked about wanting to become a Christian and now, I really think I'm in over my head. I don't know what to do." Penny hating to admit she didn't know something, knows she has to say something.

Anger, and concern flash over the devil's face. His concern was losing to the angel, not losing the demons, more just losing.

The devil quickly made an announcement to the class. "No more visits to the chapel. You all need to remember, as I told Penny a while back, there is a masquerading class and they can make you think that their angels. Don't get fooled. It may cost you your immortality. You will go from the torturer to the tortured, forever! I'm afraid I'm going to have to forbid you all from going back to the chapel."

Penny now feels horrible. Feelings are new and she does not like them. She may have gotten Despair in trouble. Despair would actually spend eternity being tortured because Penny didn't tell her about the angel and what the devil had said to her when she first encountered the angel. Penny realizes she should have told her fellow demons sooner. Her problem, she knows, is that she likes having information the other demons didn't.

Penny realizes her daydreaming, which she was not supposed to be doing, caused a problem. She lost focus during Wrath's speech. She scolds herself that it is important to always remember what you're supposed to be doing and at all times be ready to shine. She was so busy admonishing herself to pay attention, she didn't notice Wrath approaching.

Penny upon seeing Wrath, quickly says, "I'm really sorry I was daydreaming. I was just thinking you were nice looking..."

"No you weren't. You were thinking I'm angry all the time"

Penny looks at Wrath and says, "Isn't that kind of your deal? Isn't that kind of who you're supposed to be?"

"Yeah, and don't you forget it." With that, he walked away.

The devil puts himself in Despair's mind and says, "I'm sorry to have to forbid the chapel and to tell you the angel that you've seen, may be from our masquerading class. In all honesty, I don't know if the angel you met in the chapel was someone from the masquerading class."

Despair looked down and sniffled.

———

Greetings reader, so clearly a problem is developing that is a lot more involved than I originally gave it credit.

Chapter 16 Fallon 3

The devil walks through the door marked 13 - 18 in the college and immediately walks into his office in Schomolance Academy in Hell. Waiting for him is Fallon, who is holding the entire bottle of bourbon. Fallon immediately hands it to the devil and says, "It's wonderful to have you back so soon sir, but to what do I owe the pleasure?"

The devil takes a long drink directly from the bottle and explains, "Well let's see, I had one of my demons, Despair, decide to go to the chapel and want to convert to Christianity, which scared my favorite demon, Penny. Now Penny's all worried that she did something wrong by not telling everyone that she's been in contact with an angel this entire time. I think I've diffused the situation. Fallon stops straightening the devil's office and immediately turns his attention to the devil.

"First, I forbid any of the demons from going back to the chapel. I know you can't put the horse back in the barn, but I'm hoping to at least stop any other horses from leaving the barn.

"As for the angel, Penny apparently had kept it to herself this entire time. Fortunately when she first told me of the angel, I mentioned that we have an entire masquerading department and said for all she knows it's one of the demons pretending to be an angel."

Fallon gives a silent nod in agreement.

"Thankfully the Bible in Corinthians, chapter 11 verses 14 and 15 basically explains that yeah we imitate angels when necessary. I knew Penny would know this because well she's, Penny. She knows her bible.

"Everyone is already on guard that we masquerade because, of course we do. We're not doing it in this case, which is annoying because it would be so much simpler if I was just trying to catch the demons and send them to Hell. Actually that's not a bad idea to save for future trips. Right now, I don't want to send these particular demons to Hell.

"I don't care about Despair, although I certainly don't want the other side to win." The devil points up.

"Also, I don't want to send this group to Hell. These are my elite demons. These are the ones I want to keep. One of them will be the lead soul catcher. These are the best of the best. I'm not looking to get rid of one of these demons.

"Of course, now, I have this stupid angel, who has decided to come down from Heaven and try to get a couple of my demons. Obviously, I can't allow that to happen. I even had to go so far as to compliment Despair and make her believe I gave a crap about her, which I don't, but I need to keep up my charade. Despair might be having a good thought about me; or, at least questioning whether the angel is legitimate. That's the best I can do at this point

"For some reason, this angel, is trying to change the game. A game, I have successfully played countless times."

Fallon looks at the devil and says, "So how are the demons doing in this lead soul catcher position?" Hoping a change in subject, may cheer up the devil.

The devil sighs and says, "Well, Lust did a good job of attracting people and holding their interest. She really is only good for one thing. She's great at that one thing, but she's only good for one thing.

"Avarice, as you know, is my lead dog at the moment. He seems to be able to bring together the other departments. He knows what he's doing. He should be doing great, he's been through this before. Still he has a bit of a finesse, about him now. I have high hopes there.

"Gluttony, oh my goodness, was that horrible. I mean seriously, that demon is afraid of his own shadow. He is always hiding behind something, if it's not food, it is some crazy desire, about something. He couldn't even finish his speech. He gets so wrapped up in himself, no wonder he never looks at another person. It's a shame really because addiction brings us so many souls, but you can't rely on someone who is addicted, which ironically is why we get so many souls from addiction.

"Sloth did better than I expected. Again he doesn't care about anything, which is perfect for sloth. Their trademark is their apathy. He is not a go getter which means, I have no go getter to be my go getter of souls. He doesn't really want to be lead soul catcher anyway, so there's no big loss there.

"Next we heard from Envy. She's just scary. I mean I'm the devil and I'm a little afraid of her. I'm utterly amazed at all she's done, but I'm still not convinced I want to be working with her. I can't trust her that's for damn sure. I could see her in a secondary position, maybe, but yeah, I can't be having her as the second most important person down here. That is just a rebellion waiting to happen and if anyone knows about rebellion."

Fallon gave a little chuckle.

"The class listened to Wrath today. Wrath is aggressive. Oh, and he came at Penny. He can't be coming after Penny. I can't let him hurt my Penny, she's my pride. He had Penny cowering in the corner. I had to literally protect Penny from him and I can't be put in a position, where I start feeling the need to protect my demons."

Fallon wants to say his demons should be able to protect themselves, but determines it is better to not say it. Also he mentally notes, Penny means a lot to the devil and to not disparage her in any way. He now knows what side to be on in any situation where Penny is mentioned.

The devil continues, "I don't know, something was weird, there. I just, I'm not saying Wrath couldn't do it. It's just, even I didn't really want to work with his energy. He can turn on a dime. He might harm me in the process.

"The problem is there are so few deadly sins that have good leadership abilities. What makes great as a sin, makes the demon horrible as a leader. What makes Gluttony good as a sin, makes him terrible as a leader. No reliability. Lust is only good for one thing. What makes Envy good at being a sin, makes her really untrustworthy as a leader. Sloth doesn't care, so he doesn't want to lead. Wrath is uncontrollable. I think, I can work with Avarice.

"The only demons left to give their presentations, are Despair and Pride. This is a rule God insisted upon. Everybody's got to give their speech. I don't know why that was one of his rules. I just know that it was one of his rules. It didn't seem like that big of a deal, but now it means I can't just take all my demons back to Hell and declare a lead soul catcher. I have to let everyone speak or I cannot choose a lead soul catcher from this group, unless they all want to do the whole mortal on Earth thing again. Even I can't believe, Avarice was willing to do this more than once.

"Whatever, so Despair has to give her speech, Pride has to give her speech, and then, I can make my decision of who's the lead soul catcher."

Fallon finally says, "All right, so, as I see it, we kind of know who's in the lead for lead soul catcher. As long as, we don't lose any of your demons, then we can be wrapping this up in a couple of days. God doesn't have a time limit on you right?"

"No, as long as everybody gets to speak, or is unable to give the their speech because they're dead, that's his only concern. I still don't know why it's his concern, but it is. Everybody gets to speak.

"You're right. We can wrap this up in a couple of days and then I can put this nonsense behind me. I've forbidden the chapel, so none of the demons are going to go back. I've planted seeds of doubt, powerful seeds of doubt in Penny, who was already questioning, whether she was on board to convert to Christianity.

"I'm just not concerned about Penny. I have a few other aces up my sleeve if I need to pull one out to ensure she comes back. I can promise her anything. I'm the devil. I can make all kinds of empty promises, that's what I do.

"As for Despair, I really don't want to lose a demon to the other side. If I have to lose a demon, then Despair would be the least objectionable for me to lose. Honestly, she never makes it this far anyway, but still I am not happy to lose one to the other side. Usually, we lose her to our own side.

119

"I mean it's one thing when one of the demons dies while they're mortal and hasn't accepted Christ, it's another to have them convert and have Christ win. I don't want to lose."

"Well, sir, at least you were smart enough to have the demons remain on Earth so you can show that startup angel that you are smarter, stronger, and better than her. You were smart enough to forbid the chapel because the demons aren't at your level. They're not smart enough to not get suckered in by the other side. You were smart to have Penny and Despair question whether the angel is from our side or Heaven's side. No, I like our chances. I am sure you'll do well or our team will do well." Fallon hopes his pep talk relaxes and encourages the devil.

Chapter 17 Despair

Despair crosses the street. She is coming back from the chapel. She didn't care that the devil told her not to go. She wanted to go and she didn't bring Penny so it's not like he would care. With all of this running through her mind, she didn't look before crossing the street. The bus driver didn't look in time either.

———

Sloth hadn't felt right all night, or when he woke up in the morning. His hair is a mess and his clothes are all wrinkled, like he had slept in them. He walks into the lecture hall, the other demons are already in their seats. Wrath yells, "Sloth, you look bad, even for you. What's the matter?"

Sloth answers, "I don't know. I just don't feel right. Maybe I'm getting a cold. I really don't want a mortal cold. I hate being mortal. I want to go back to where we don't get sick. This whole being mortal thing sucks. I prefer being a demon, where we have less feelings." Sloth takes his seat, just in time for the devil to arrive.

He walks in from the top doors of the lecture hall, down to the podium, like he did on the first day. Everyone is turning, staring, they can tell he has an important announcement. The demons could feel it in the energy of the room.

"I'm sure you've heard by now, Despair is dead," the devil says. The room is silent. The demons don't say anything and have stunned looks on their faces.

"Wait, what, Despair is dead?" Envy asks with a smile. She is a little too happy to have the number of people in the competition decrease.

"When did this happen?" asks Sloth.

"According to campus security, she was hit by a bus, sometime last night. Interesting how Dante writes a book saying 'abandon all hope, ye who enter here' talking about Hell and Despair doesn't die until she comes to Earth. I guess now, she really has no hope."

Penny asks, "Did she die a demon? Is she going to go to Hell? Did she die a Christian? What happens to her?" She was so shocked at the news. It never occurred to her that the devil might be

lying. He certainly could and would lie, but not this time. Despair was dead.

"How would I know? I've been up here the whole time. I'm sure she is being processed, likely in Hell, but even if she managed to become a Christian and be saved, she would still have to be processed and judged. Like I said, I've been up here the whole time. I really don't know what's going on. I am not omniscient," answers the devil.

Penny says, "I have another question that will seem really off topic, but when Dante says 'abandon all hope, ye who enter here' doesn't that conflict with the Apostles' Creed that says Jesus went back down to Hell? I mean wouldn't there always be a reason to hope?"

"That's it Penny, way to worry about Despair. You are as bad as the rest of us, but, for some reason, you think you're above us. You're not. You are just like the rest of us," says Avarice.

"I know that's not what we're talking about, but I've always wondered about it and I don't know when the opportunity will come back again to ask. So what about hope in Hell?" Penny directs her question back to the devil, and then stares at Avarice.

The devil is happy to see Penny's inquisitive mind winning out over the emotional side. The last thing he wanted, was for her to consider her fellow demon. He liked it better, when she just thought about the facts. Things that can make her forget her fellow man. He was very happy to answer this question. "That is a great question, Penny. I'm afraid I can't tell you what was going through the mind of an Italian poet back in the early 1300s. Also, it's a work of fiction, so I don't know how to answer."

"Is there any hope in Hell?" Penny asks completely forgetting the point the devil made when he walked in the room, that Despair was dead.

"You've been there. Have you ever seen any? There is no hope for the damned. They've already been judged, but really, I'm just the devil, what do I know?"

"All right. Obviously Despair is not going to be able to give her speech about her sin. So I'll give you the rundown," begins the devil.

Wrath interrupts the devil, "Why bother telling us about Despair? She's dead. She isn't even a deadly sin. She is no longer in the running for lead soul catcher. Why should we care?"

The devil answers, "Well, to be honest, I don't care either, but God had some rules that I had to agree to, before I was allowed to bring demons up to Earth. One of the rules is that every demon gets to or has to explain their sin. She can't explain her sin, so I'm going to explain it. This is a precaution so God can't say this trip doesn't count. No one wants to repeat this right. Well, except you Avarice. You seem to be racking up frequent flyer miles, although you do improve with each trip, I must say."

Avarice smiles.

Gluttony asks, "What do you mean, do this again? Avarice mentioned once that he had done it before. And what do you mean God's permission? Can you just tell us what's going on?"

The devil smiles and says, "Oh, we've been going through this for as long as I can remember. Anytime I need to replace the lead soul catcher, I have to send a group of elite demons up to Earth and put you at risk of dying, but in exchange I get smarter at getting souls and I get better demons. I suppose it is a little unfair you have no idea about the risk or that Despair is often a casualty."

Gluttony asks, "So we're all just on an endless loop?"

"Well, yes and no. I mean the embodiments of your sins are on an endless loop. You each individually represent a deadly sin. Those representations keep repeating, but the individuals who represent the sins change. Am I making any sense? Oh well, it doesn't matter. The point is I've done this numerous times. I'm going to continue to do this time and time again. Now, I'm getting tired of this conversation so I'm just going to start discussing the sin of despair."

The demons looked at one another not happy with the explanation, but they understood their lot. They know they could push the devil no further. While it's always better to be the torturer instead of the tortured, that doesn't mean it's easy to be the torturer.

The devil continues, "The sin of despair or despondence separates the mortal from Christ. It is why the sin started as a deadly sin. Despair is you don't believe you're good enough, ever, or you believe you are so low that God himself does not have the capacity to forgive you. This means you're questioning the abilities of God. God can save anyone and everyone, theoretically.

"God could even save one of you demons. He is powerful enough to do it, but he probably wouldn't. Let's face it, you demons are pretty committed to your sins and to our side." The demons smile.

The devil continues, "If you weren't as good as you are, in your respective sins, you wouldn't be in this class, being taught by yours truly.

"Despair's life was pretty sad. She was constantly second guessing herself. She had a melancholy way about her, even when some other students, yeah I'm looking at you Penny, took her out to try and cheer her up. Many tried to suggest you're just going through a bad patch.

"She still didn't feel like she was good enough, that she was ever going to measure up. She could never get the big jock, like Wrath, or the flashy guy, like Avarice. She never felt she could do any of these things.

"It is often said envy is one of the saddest deadly sins because that sin never gets to enjoy what they have. Lust enjoys the attention and the act. Avarice enjoys what he gets. Envy doesn't enjoy it because she is always about comparison.

"Despair doesn't believe she deserves anything. So even if she was the smartest, the brightest, the prettiest, she wouldn't see it. She doesn't understand it, even if someone says she's cute. She's just gonna say 'oh, thanks' and not believe the other person. She's a dark gray cloud.

"There is talk of an unforgivable sin, which is to blaspheme the Holy Spirit, which is difficult for a Christian to do. It doesn't mean insulting the Holy Spirit. What it really means is, you don't believe in the Holy Spirit's ability. The holy spirit is necessary for Jesus to have been created by God, yet, born mortal, and have the power of God. If a mortal doesn't believe that, then they are not a Christian.

"If you're a Christian, you believe in the father, the son, and the Holy Spirit; the Holy Trinity. If you don't believe in Jesus Christ, you're not a Christian, obviously. If you believe that Christ was the son of God, you have to believe in the Holy Spirit.

"If you don't believe in someone's existence, it gets pretty hard for them to save you.

"For instance, I don't particularly believe in the blue hippopotamus with pink spots, that comes by and gives people ice cream. So, I promise you to this day, I have not been handed an ice cream by a blue hippopotamus with pink spots.

"Despair didn't believe anyone would think she was worth saving or that anyone could save her. She didn't believe in the Holy Spirit."

Penny, in the back of the room, looks down. She knows the devil was correct. If you didn't believe, you were worth saving or that someone was capable of saving you, then there was no chance of you being saved.

She missed her friend. She never really had a friend, but she guesses Despair was a friend. It is hard to think of someone who was always sad and depressing to be around as a friend. Regardless, she missed her friend.

Wrath asks, "We are already in Hell. Where is she going to go?"

The devil answers, "That's the best part. You're already in Hell. You can't go anywhere else, so don't worry. Despair's not going anywhere, really. Honestly, she was sad before and she'll be sad now. There really wasn't a change, not geographically, not mood wise. I mean she's obviously not in this class anymore and she's gonna be tortured.

"We're here to take souls, we are not here to make friends. I know, Penny, she was kind of a friend but I guess it's time you learn not everyone's gonna make it. You're going to lose some, even as a demon."

"All right, class is dismissed. I have a lot of paperwork to do in my office so I can't stay behind today." With that, he quickly turns and walks out the door.

Sloth follows very quickly out the door behind him.

———

The rest of the class goes to the cafeteria. Once there, Avarice says, "Really, this happens every time."

Everyone turns and looks at him, like what do you mean this happens every time.

He says, "Like the devil said, this is not my first time being here. I have put my soul on the line before. So this time, I am damn sure going to get lead soul catcher. Despair never makes it to the end, although, this is as far as I've ever seen her get."

"Did she ever go into the chapel on the other trips?" asks Penny.

"No, I don't think so, but it's not like I cared enough to notice," said Avarice.

"I would just like to say I for one am not happy that you have been here before," Envy says looking at Avarice. Turning toward Penny, Envy continues, "And you have been talking to an angel. It seems like you're both getting extra help and that this isn't a fair fight. I'm not saying I want a fair fight, unless I'm the one getting the advantage. I just don't want you two getting extra help."

Wrath chimes in, "I agree this isn't a fair fight."

Penny leaves thinking to herself, 'This was not part of the plan.' She slowly walks back to her dorm.

Chapter 18 Fallon 4

Fallon pushes the entire liquor cart into the devil's office. He is waiting for the devil.

On the other side of the door marked 13-18, the devil is pushing the door and not noticing that Sloth is coming in right behind him. Back in Hell, Sloth returns to his immortal state.

Fallon gives a motion of his head to the devil indicating he should look behind him. The devil is shocked to see a very tired and worn Sloth in his office in Hell.

The devil turns and angrily says, "What are you doing here? Why did you follow me? You're not ready to come back to Hell."

Sloth looks at the devil and says, "I can't take it anymore. These emotions are just too much for me. I'm used to being separated from Despair. She's been separated from me for centuries, but there is still kind of a connection between us, or at least there used to be. I don't know, just knowing Despair's gone really hurts. I can't go back to Earth. I get it. I'm not going to be lead soul catcher, that's fine. I understand I am not your top pick. Let's face it, I was never going to be your top pick. I'm far too relaxed and I don't care enough to be your top pick. I am not Avarice. I am not Envy. I'm not Penny. I'm certainly not Penny.

"I know who I am. I know where I stand, and I know I can't stand Earth anymore. Please just let me return back to Hell."

The devil looks at Sloth and doesn't know what to do with him. It's not like sympathy is the devil's strong point; however, he is concerned that he's losing. He doesn't need anything else to worry about. He may have lost a demon, he doesn't want to lose any more, and the thought of getting to have one safe and sound in Hell is probably not a bad idea. He looks at Sloth and says, "Fine, I don't care, just go. Just get out of this office, go back to your normal position in Hell. I've had too much going on today, just go."

Sloth moves faster than he's ever moved. No longer mortal, he goes out the door on the other side of the devil's office, which opens directly into Hell, screams of the tortured can be heard.

Fallon looks to the devil and says, "So I'm guessing you're not back for pleasure. What happened up there?"

"Despair is dead. I don't know where her soul went." The devil takes a drink from the liquor cart, looks at Fallon, and says "Despair always dies during this yes, but I'm not sure if Despair became a Christian and accepted Christ before she died. So, first order of business, has Despair come through central processing. Did I lose her or is she somewhere still in our processing?"

Fallon looks at the devil and says, "Well, it's a bureaucracy and this is Hell, so, I have absolutely no idea. We probably aren't going to know for quite a long time. If she's being processed in Heaven, it's probably going to take a while before they know whether she belongs up there or belongs down here. So, it's going to be hell on that end too. I'm just assuming there's a bureaucracy. There always is. She's not the only one who died today.

"So what else is going on that has you concerned?"

The devil says, "I'm a little worried, I'm losing Penny more and more. Everybody was upset at Despair being killed. She was hit by a bus."

"Well that's a new one. I don't think we've lost one that way before. Seriously, was looking both ways too hard?" Fallon jokes, hoping to cheer up the devil.

"I know, right." The devil chuckles. "Anyway, Penny took it a lot worse than I was expecting. Penny has told the other demons about being approached by an angel. Basically, they all know way more, than they should know.

"I thought my stop gap measure of asking them, 'how do they know the being they saw wasn't just someone masquerading as an angel.' was going to be enough.

"I'm concerned. I really think I lost Despair," the devil confesses to Fallon, who nods, and gives an understanding smile.

"I think the angel took Despair or that Despair converted to Christianity because the other times Despair died; it was very obvious she was going to Hell. I have never seen her go into the chapel before. I have never seen this angel before. I just seem to be losing control over my demons this time."

Fallon, trying to calm the devil down, says, "Ok, I doubt it's as serious as all that. Maybe, it's a case of she went up to Heaven; she has to go through their central processing; and they haven't realized she's a demon, yet. They're going to realize 'Hey you're a demon. You can't go to Heaven.' She's going to get kicked down in a little while. Then, she has to go through our internal processing, which is going to take a while. I'll call down and ask. I'll tell them the devil wants to know, that should scare them into action. I will let you know as soon as I know. I'm not as worried about it as you are. I'm sure this will get resolved quickly." Fallon goes back to tidying up the devil's office.

The devil, slumps in his office chair, not quite ready to move along back to Earth. He wants to spend a few more minutes in Hell, where he is in charge.

He turns to Fallon and says, "Part of me wants to take the rest of my demons back to hell, to just forget the unpleasantness of this visit ever happened."

Fallon looks at the devil with an expression of understanding, but then tilts his head to the side.

The devil looking at Fallon says, "You're right. I know what I'll do. I can't give up. I need to offer Penny a great deal, one she can't turn down. Her pride won't let her."

"I knew you'd come up with the right answer, sir," says Fallon.

Chapter 19 Penny Feels Vulnerable

When she gets to her dorm she slumps down to the ground, wraps her arms around her knees, and lets everything sink in. Then, the angel appears and Penny calms down. It was like the hamster on the wheel got to take a break, got to breathe for a few seconds, and stop running. Finally, Penny turns, not really being able to see the angel, at first, but then she could see the angel more clearly than she ever could.

Penny says, "What, what is this?"

The angel says, "I am here to tell you, how good it can be? How you can stop this endless need to feel achievement, to get things done, to just relax, and take a breath. You're going to need to let go and let God. It's ridiculously hard, but once you do it, you'll be at peace.

"I know you're someone who likes to be in complete control at all times, but let go. It will be fine," the angel says.

Penny shoots back, "It's not going to be fine. It's never going to be fine, my friend is dead. And I don't even know if I have friends."

The angel continues to soothe Penny's soul. Penny exhales for the first time in quite a long time. In fact, it might have been the first time, she ever really exhaled. Penny has a calm breath, where everything is ok.

Penny not being able to be still any longer asks "Did she die a demon? Is she going to go to Hell? Did she die a Christian? What happened to Despair?"

"That is not up to me," answers the angel.

"Well you're an angel, can't you go up there and do a roll call see if she's there?"

"I could, but the whole point is, you need to have faith. I can't tell you yes or no, you have to have faith," says the angel.

"Despair had to have enough faith to get over her feeling of unworthiness to be saved. I can't tell you whether demons can get into Heaven. The question will be, did Despair believe whether God could save her."

Penny says, "The devil brought up a few other points that concerned me a lot."

The angel nods with her eyebrows raised to indicate to Penny "Go on. What did he say?"

"All right. I'm just going to say these things in no particular order because I need to get them all out.

"First, are you just another demon masquerading as an angel, not that you would tell me if you were a demon masquerading as an angel? How do I know you're legit?

"Second, the devil mentioned something about blaspheming the Holy Spirit and that it's unforgivable. So if I'm operating under something that's unforgivable, why am I trying to be forgiven, since I can't be."

The angel takes a deep breath and says, "Ok, let me answer the first part about am I a demon masquerading as an angel. Ultimately that's going to be a faith question, for you. I can't answer it in any way, you will believe. Like you said, if I were a demon, I would lie. Since I'm not a demon, I'm going to answer that I'm not a demon masquerading as an angel.

"I realize that doesn't answer your question. Very simply, it is kind of an unanswerable question"

Penny nods. She isn't happy with the answer but she understands why the angel really couldn't answer the question.

The angel continues, "Let me touch upon your second point, about blaspheming the Holy Spirit. First, I have to tell you, the devil lies. It's what he does. In this case, he didn't explain things completely. He gave you, as he often does, a rough overview of the situation, your mortal brain filled in the rest.

The angel continues, "To blaspheme the Holy Spirit, it must be intentional and it must be declared, usually verbally. Let me ask, at any point in time, did you say the words 'I do not believe in the Holy Spirit or similarly there is no Holy Spirit?'

Penny answers, "No."

"Ok, then, I don't think you've blasphemed the Holy Spirit. I think you're uneducated, didn't know there was a Holy Spirit, or the extent of God's power. In Despair's case, she didn't understand the true power of God, not understanding something, is very different from not believing in something. Not knowing of something's existence is not the same as not believing. Let's face it, in human existence, there were a great many years where people didn't know dinosaurs existed. People thought they were myths. They now have fossils. They can see proof that they existed. Now that's a case that does not call for faith. The Holy Spirit is a case that calls for faith. It's going to come down to, do you have faith? You can't come to that decision, if you have never been educated about God's power," says the angel.

Penny replies, "Here is my concern. I am a damn good demon. I am in the running to be lead soul catcher. I have a real good chance of being lead soul catcher. This a big deal. I have wanted it all my life. I know how Hell works and I am on track to be doing pretty darn well there. I don't even know if Despair went to Heaven or if any demon can go to Heaven. I actually don't even know if you are an angel. Can you give me any thing more than I have to have faith?"

The angel answers, "No, you have to have faith in all of this. I will say, if you weren't a little bit intrigued, I wouldn't still be here and you wouldn't still be listening."

Chapter 20 A Great Deal

Penny is sitting alone in the library. The devil walks over and sits across from her. He says, "You seem kind of sad. What's going on?"

Penny looks at the devil and says, "There is a lot going on. I'm trying to sort it all out. Also I need to give my presentation, which, I know is due tomorrow.

"I don't want to screw up my presentation. I don't want to make anything I have done or seen, in the last few days, make you believe that I am not 100% committed to being lead soul catcher.

"I'm not sure what's going on and I know that I can't simply ask this angel 'are you an angel?' because if she is an angel, she'll, of course, say 'yes' and if she's a masquerading demon, she will, of course, say 'yes'.

"I understand this is going to come down to a me question and what I believe. I guess, I'll ask your advice, if you don't mind."

The devil looks over, rather impressed that someone wants his opinion, and says, "Well of course dear, how can I help? What would you like to know?"

Penny says, 'How do you know when someone's lying? I mean you're the father of lies. How do you know, for sure, when someone's lying? Because I think I need help in this area." Penny hates to admit it, but she needs help.

The devil looks at her and says, "Well it's not always easy. Obviously, on some things my job is very simple. I know someone's lying, if a little kid is covered in chocolate cake and says, 'I didn't eat the chocolate cake.' Yeah, I can see very easily that you ate the chocolate cake. So, I can see through simple ones like that.

"Let's look at this angel. Let me play devil's advocate, a me advocate, if you will. This will be fun.

"All right, let's start with did she tell you what you're gonna do in Heaven all day? I mean I know what we do in Hell. You must know, too. Oh I'm all aflutter, no one ever intentionally asks my advice.

"I'm assuming since you're a demon, you were raised in Hell. You know the rules of the game. You are a very good demon. Of course, you had a good teacher, if I do say so myself."

Penny says, "I know, I'm a really good demon. I know the rules and how to play the game. I don't know why this angel is bothering me. Unless, is this a test? Am I in danger of failing the test because I didn't realize the angel is actually from the masquerading class, even though you told me? Is this like a loyalty test, and if it is, am I failing?"

The Devil smiles and says, "I can't tell you, but that is an interesting question." He liked that she was not trusting of the angel.

He continues, "Back to the situation at hand, what's the angel offering? Do you know what it's like in Heaven?"

"No. The closest I've come is the chapel," says Penny.

"Ok, the closest you've come is the chapel. I'm assuming it was a good feeling, yes, very calm. Ok, do you just get to sit around and be calm all day? Or what do you do?"

"I-I don't know ."

"Ok so you have to give up what you know, what you can do, and what you're really skilled at for a complete unknown. Has she guaranteed you that demons can get in to Heaven?"

"No, she hasn't. She has neither, guaranteed me that I can get in; nor, has she guaranteed me that demons can get in to Heaven. Yeah, let's face it, we all represent deadly sins. I'm pretty happy with pride. I don't understand why I'm even considered a sin."

"Neither do I," says the devil with a little chuckle.

The devil continues, "Don't worry. I am not holding any of this against you. I understand you're in a precarious situation. I've got a demon from the masquerading class doing an impeccable job and they're doing what they should do. You are looking at it and examining it like you should do. I don't want a dumb lead soul catcher."

Penny looks up at the devil and says, "Am I going to be the lead soul catcher?"

"It's looking that way, but I'm not omniscient, even I don't know, what I'm going to do. It is looking pretty good, dear. I, also, can't say that, because I have to keep everything fair and pick out the lead soul catcher at the end of the class. So, I have to hear your presentation as well, but it's looking pretty good.

"I liked that you looked after the other demons. Being able to control the other demons is going to be necessary. Being able to interact with all kinds is going to be necessary. All in all, I need a well-rounded demon and the fact that you are looking at everything critically tells me that you're a well-rounded demon. I understand that you're looking at and evaluating all the information. Now, while you're evaluating all of this information, let me just remind you, that you do still have to give your presentation tomorrow. I'd also like to know by tomorrow, who won. I need to know with 100% certainty. Did the angel win or did I win? Are you going with the angel or are you going with me and your fellow demons back home to Hell?"

Penny looks at the devil and says, "I never looked at it so cut and dry but I guess it really is. Am I following a potential masquerading demon to an unknown destination to do who knows what, or am I returning to Hell, my home, with the devil and the demons I have always known?

"I feel like I am being foolish to follow a masquerading demon. Wow, when you put it that way, I appreciate the position I'm in and it's a scary one. As I said, sir, please don't take anything that's going on here as a mark against my commitment toward Hell and catching souls"

The devil smiles and waves away her concerns and says, "I've never worried at all, Penny. The whole point of having you demons come up to Earth and live as mortals is for you to understand what they go through. They are all going to have these concerns. What I need is for you to be able to talk with the mortals; reason with them; and get them to see our side. So I need you to be able to show me you can make this decision yourself.

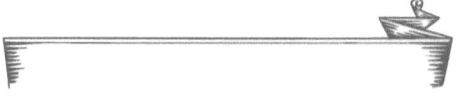

Chapter 21 Realization

Penny walks into the cafeteria. Exhausted from the night before, she barely slept a wink, she sees the other demons. She has known them all her life. She doesn't know if she would call them friends, but they were certainly what she had known for as long as she could remember. It feels odd to even think about leaving them or the way of existence she had always known, but she also knows that she really doesn't fit in with them anymore.

She walks over to the table, where everyone is seated and says, "Hi."

The other demons look at Penny and can see that her night has been rough.

Lust says, "Hi, what's the matter with you? You should be on top of the world. I know Despair died and you spent a lot of time with her, but we are nearing the end of the big selection process. We all kind of know the devil likes you and as usual you're kind of knocking it out of the park. Really, all you have to do is deliver your last speech. Why would you possibly have a reason to feel bad with all this going your way?"

Penny looks at everyone and says, "It's Despair; it's the angel; and it's everything that's been going on. I guess I just don't feel 100%."

Lust looks at Penny with her special gaze and says, "Would you like me to get you some chocolate cake?"

Penny very quickly answers, "No, I'm good thanks."

Avarice looks at her and says, "You never did fit in with the rest of us. If you're looking to fit in, that's probably not going to happen. You've always felt you were better than the rest of us. You seem unable to accept that you're a demon. I hate to admit it, but your kind of good at being a demon. You just seem to not want to be good at it."

Envy looks at Penny and says, "Yeah, not only are you good at it, you've got some hidden connection with an angel, totally unfair. I don't feel I should have to compete with someone who's getting secondary insight or has an in with the other side. I definitely think the devil is helping you or likes you more than me. I'm not happy about it, at all. So frankly, I'm glad you're having a bad day. It makes my day look better."

Wrath looks at Penny and says, "Look, I just don't want any more interruptions like we had with this Despair incident. If you're going to do something weird; just do it. Get it over with, so we can get back to Hell. I got people I need to see."

Penny looks at Wrath and says, "Oh I'm sorry, is the death of my friend an inconvenience for you?"

Wrath replies, "Yeah, it is. It interrupted things. It has the devil acting weird and put all the attention on you. I need the attention to be off of you and on me. Also, we are demons. We don't have friends."

Penny rolls her eyes.

Gluttony then asks, "Hey, does anybody know where Sloth is?"

The demons all looked at each other and shake their heads no.

Avarice says, "No, I haven't seen him since we heard about Despair. He's probably just sleeping somewhere." The demons all kind of look at each other and agree. Not one of them exhibiting any concern that one of them was missing.

Penny can't believe that one of this weird family sort of dynamic, she had, is missing and not one of them cares. She, too, then put it aside.

Finally Gluttony, usually in his own little world, looks at her and says, "I am sure everything will be fine. You'll do what you do best, which is explain pride, show all of us up, and we will return to Hell, as the demons we are."

Even though Penny is surrounded by the demons she had known all her life, she didn't feel like she fit in and for once, she didn't feel like she was better than the other demons. She just knows, she doesn't feel the same as the other demons. She just knows this is not where she belongs.

————

Penny looks across the cafeteria and sees the angel sitting alone at a table far away. She leaves the demons and walks over to the angel.

The angel says, "Hi, it's nice to see you. Everything going well?"

Penny answers, "No everything is not going well. I don't belong with the group I have known all my life. I don't know how else to explain it, but I don't feel anything like I used to feel. It used to be, I would see the demons I've known all my life and I knew I was at the top of the pecking order. I knew, I knew more than the rest of them. I knew I was better than them and now I just don't feel that connection. It's not that I feel I'm better than them. It's that I don't feel a connection. It's that I look at their behaviors and I guess I'm judging, but it's more. I'm looking at their behaviors and saying I don't want to do this anymore. I don't want to be part of this group anymore.

"So now, I have nowhere to go. I'm guessing, I'm not just going to fit in with angels. I, now, just feel lost."

The angel looks at Penny and says, "You're growing that's what humans do. You're mortal right now. So you pretty much are human. You have just grown beyond the demons, you knew. You can tell this because you care about, well, anything other than yourself. When you were a demon and you represented pride you only cared about yourself. What makes pride bad is when it turns into you only thinking of yourself.

"The humility that pride needs is not thinking less of yourself, but thinking of yourself less. Remember back to Gluttony when he left the room, he just left. You, and only you, went to check on him. You, and only you, seemed to care about Despair. Sloth when he got any feelings, he had to leave Earth completely and return to Hell. You stayed. You're growing as a mortal. This means you aren't going to fit in with the demons you used to spend time with. You aren't who you used to be.

"Lust doesn't care about anybody. She made that very clear in her speech. Avarice doesn't care about anybody. He just wants more. Wrath certainly doesn't care about anybody. Envy cares about everybody, but in a very different way than you would like or expect. Gluttony is too preoccupied to care about anybody and Sloth very flatly does not care about anybody.

"You, Penny, care about everybody or at least are starting to and that separates you from the other demons. You say you don't fit in with them anymore, it's because you care, they don't. What you choose to do with that feeling and whether you want to continue to have that feeling, is really the big question. Do you want to continue to care about people or do you want to damn them to Hell?

"Also I'm reasonably certain that a masquerading demon, wouldn't break it down for you in this manner." With that, the angel got up from the cafeteria table and walked away.

———

Envy comes up to Penny and says, "I can sense that you are envious of the calmness of the other demons. We know who we are. We know who we serve. We don't have any delusions of even considering the other side. I know you're going through some existential crisis and you somehow think you're better than us, like you'll be able to be the one demon saved by Christ but understand this: I can't wait for you to go from nearly the boss of me to someone I get to torture. I can't wait to tell the devil of your current crisis. I am sure that will affect his view of his perfect Penny." She walks away leaving Penny feeling lost.

———

Only a few minutes later, the devil walks up to Penny and says, "I see you're talking to the other demons, that's good. Maybe getting you back around those, you have known your entire life, will help you know where you belong."

Penny answers, "Yeah I'm beginning to learn where I do and don't belong."

The devil looks at her quizzically and says, "Oh, do you not feel like you belong with us? Do you suddenly feel like you're better than us? Let me explain something to you, my dear, the point of this excursion to Earth was to make the demons better at catching souls. The demon should improve at catching souls; not at being mortal.

"The entire time that we have been up here, like all mortals, because again while you're up here you're mortal, and like all mortals, you only see what you want to see and you only hear what you want to hear. I told you that early on, when I explained your mortality. I doubt you'll remember, most mortals don't recognize that they only hear what they want to hear and see what they want to see. This is how I'm able to get so many mortals. They don't think about other people, they don't realize how their actions affect others.

"In your case, I needed to make you feel comfortable around me. I needed to have you see me as a mentor, a parental figure, if you will. Do you really think that I sound like this? I am the ruler of Hell. Do you think I use words like 'skedaddle'?

"Do you think I'm this kind, caring, father like figure that appeared to be in your head? This whole time you've portrayed me as some kind of mentor; that's nice, that's interesting. If that's the shtick you want me to play; great, no problem. I probably can get a lot of souls like this, because I would totally be under the radar, but that's not who I am.

"As for you only seeing what you want to see, your mortal form is a bit of a prude. The first day of presentations when Lust was speaking; what you saw was a kiss, what actually happened was sex, in front of the whole class.

"Wrath and I went a couple of rounds. You didn't see that either, did you? You can rewrite history all you want, rewrite the present, all mortals do it. I just need you to be aware that you did it." Penny had to admit to herself that she really only saw the kiss and an intense conversation. In mortal form she did only see what she wanted to see and hear what you wanted to hear.

"I can see that something's changed in you, Penny. I just need to remind you that yeah, you aren't who you were when all of this started, and to a certain degree that's the point of sending demons to Earth. I send demons to improve at being demons. I'm sending you here to learn what it's like to be mortal so that you can get better at getting souls.

"You seem to have gotten better at seeing what you want to see and hearing what you want to hear. You got better at caring and being mortal and you were supposed to be getting better at being a demon. I can see now why you feel like you don't fit in and to be honest, I'm not sure you're gonna fit in anymore.

"Frankly, it's a lot of wasted time. A lot of wasting of my time, to think of all the demons I could have sent down here instead of you."

Penny looks down. She knows she upset the devil and she knows she doesn't fit in. Tears fill her eyes and her face is hot, but she does not let herself cry.

Chapter 22 Fallon 5

The devil quickly leaves the cafeteria and heads directly to room 13-18. He walks through the door and there is Fallon waiting for him.

Fallon did not have any kind of liquor. He is at a loss. It has been a long time since he has seen the devil like this. He is just standing there, waiting for the devil, not knowing what to do.

The devil looks at him and says, "Yep, I just completely blew it with Penny. Lost my cool, did not do what I should have done, and even worse, I alerted her to the fact that she only sees what she wants to see and that she's a prude. So, now I've completely lost two demons."

Fallon looks at the devil and says, "I doubt it's as bad as all that, sir. Why don't you tell me what was said; let's figure out how to make the best out of it; and we'll kind of go from there."

The devil looks at Fallon and says, "Well, I had to tell her she only sees what she wants to see; hears what she wants to hear; and she improved as a mortal, not as a demon. Now, I'm kind of at a loss. I truly do not know what to do.

"This isn't supposed to happen. I'm supposed to send my demons up to Earth. They improve in catching souls. I take my demons back to Hell. Everything is fine.

"Yes, I lose Despair every time, but she just dies and returns to Hell for eternal torture. I don't really lose her. She just goes from torturer to tortured soul. Either way, she is in Hell and sad. I take Despair knowing she isn't going to survive. I take Despair to Earth really just to torture her. It's just a nice new way to torture her. I don't care about her, but now this angel is taking my Penny."

Fallon nods. He knows how much it hurts the devil to lose the demon who embodies pride. "Ok, well let's look at what's going on, this is not the first time you've been down. It will not be the last time you are knocked down. If anybody is the comeback kid, it is you. Let's face it you got kicked out of Heaven and ended up the ruler of all of Hell. Let's have a little faith in ourselves."

Fallon continues, "Yes this is an unpleasant moment, but you will find your way back from this and you will live to take other demons out and get souls. Now come on, where is the devil I serve? Let me see a bit of that fire in your eyes."

The devil looks at Fallon feeling slightly better and remembers that he has been through bad times before and will go through bad times again. Although at the rate humanity is going, the devil is probably not going to have bad times for a while. The devil has to admit, he's got to let God win a few now and then.

The devil looks at Fallon, and feeling more alive says, "Ok, let's look at practical matters, every demon, but Penny, has given their speech. I've lost Despair, that was expected. I'm going to lose Penny, not happy about that, but we can deal. Sloth is already back safely in Hell. No Sloth has ever made, nor even wanted to be, lead soul catcher. So, Sloth being sent back down doesn't matter and now I have one less demon slot to fill next time.

Fallon wants to say something, but thinks better of reminding the devil that the demons can't leave early. They have to hear everyone's speech.

"I know who my lead soul catcher will be and I know who my second in command soul catcher will be. Avarice is going to win. Envy will come in second. Really what this did, was show me that it doesn't always have to be pride who wins. Avarice can win and maybe shaking things up down here in Hell will help. Maybe I will learn to get new kinds of souls. So, as much as I don't like change, maybe we have to shake things up a little bit down here.

"Envy is really really good. Envy is too good so that's why she's second. We cannot have her getting any higher up. She reminds me a little too much of me and we're not going to let that happen again. We can learn from Heaven's mistake.

"That's what we'll end up doing. All right I feel better. I have a game plan that takes into account Penny staying on Earth. If for some reason, I am wrong, which rarely happens, but let's say I'm wrong and pleasantly surprised that Penny decides she wants to come back home to Hell, then great we will welcome her with open arms.

"If that doesn't work that way, there is a game plan. We will survive and possibly thrive with this new type of soul catcher. It's always pride who becomes the gateway sin. Maybe this time, Avarice gets a chance. So we'll have Avarice and Envy. I bet you, I can get a lot of people into Hell with what essentially is greed and wanting.

HE WHO DOES NOT EXIST

"Well Fallon, see here you were at a complete and utter loss. You didn't even have a drink for me. Really, you're slipping old boy." With that the devil went back to Earth quite happy with himself.

Chapter 23 Pride

The devil walks into the classroom and says, "Ok class, our last speech is today. Let's try to make this as quick as possible. I'm sure we're all anxious to get out of here. I know I am. Penny, come give your speech."

Penny walks to the front of the room and for the first time, she's a little self-conscious. She looks at her classmates and realizes, she really doesn't know any of them, the way she should, after associating with them, for as long as she can remember. She looks at everyone and says, "Hi, I guess you know we've been through a lot in the last week or so. I know all eyes are on me to explain what's going on; explain the sin of pride; and oh yeah, explain my decision because let's face it, that's all anybody cares about.

"I'll start with explaining the sin of pride. The sin of pride has good points and bad points and people talk about it in a lot of different ways. I certainly came to appreciate it a lot more since I've been on Earth and even more by being mortal. I have to say our coming up to Earth for this leads soul catcher position selection and being turned into a mortal has truly been an eye opener. I have learned so much in such a short period of time.

"I didn't know what mortals felt and what mortals went through. I didn't expect to have this many feelings. I have to say, I had never had feelings before and now that I have them; I don't know that I'm ready to give them up. There are some good feelings, there are some bad feelings, but mostly, I know that they serve a purpose.

"Ok let me tell you about pride. I gotta say I only looked at pride as a good thing. I get my crap done. I take pride in my appearance; my knowing things; and being prepared.

"There is a thing called authentic pride. There is also hubristic pride. Essentially, authentic pride is productivity, competence, and accomplishments. That's totally me. That's what I totally thought of when I thought of pride, but my being proud of my authentic pride can easily lead to hubristic pride.

"Hubristic pride is arrogance, egotism, and conceitedness. I can freely admit I thought myself better than any mortal and definitely better than all of you.

"All of you can attest to my conceited pride. Let's face it, there were times when I was annoying. I like my confidence. I like knowing I can get everything done. I'm productive and I'm happy that I'm productive. I take pride in my accomplishments. I have worked hard to get where I am, but I also have to realize that in addition to all those things, I have probably stepped too far into hubris.

"I think it's a given, that I will be productive and accomplish things. I'm conceited about it. I don't really ever stop and think about other people. I wouldn't be where I am if it wasn't for others, like had the devil not chosen me to go up to Earth. I wouldn't have learned all these things, but my ego is sitting there saying well of course he chose me. I'm productive;

I'm confident; and I've accomplished all these things. It's kind of a catch 22.

"I know what you really want to know," says Penny. The devil looks at her raises both eyebrows and nods.

"What's going on with me? You know, I've had a tough time with Despair's death. There's been an angel and you're all wondering what I've chosen. Who I'm gonna follow?

"Basically, I started to care about Despair and how she felt. I genuinely had concern for her well-being. I never cared how someone felt, but now I care about how she feels or felt.

"She's gone. I know you're thinking Penny, you know an angel, just ask the angel if Despair is in Heaven. This is a no-brainer and Penny, your usually smart. Here's the thing, the angel won't tell me. I have asked and I won't get to know until I'm in Heaven, assuming I get to go to Heaven.

"You would think having an in with an angel, as Envy puts it, that I could tell you what happened to Despair. I can't. The angel won't tell me.

"Here is the deal, it's going to come down to faith, either I believe that she has been saved or I do not believe that she has been saved. That is it. I'll never get to know for certain, until I die and I go to Heaven, which is also not a guarantee. There is no guarantee. I will just never know, in my lifetime, and I have to be ok with not knowing." At this point the devil realizing he lost is making a wrap it up circular motion with his hand. He is done listening.

Avarice speaks from the back of the class and says, "Penny, you're insane. I don't know what you're doing. I don't know what happened to you, while you were here, but speaking as someone who has known you for many, many years, and knows how much all of this means to you, you are seriously not thinking straight. Right now, you are about to give up, pretty much a guarantee of everything you've ever wanted, for nothing. You understand that on the other side of the equation of you getting everything you ever wanted is nothing, right? I think you need to stop, take a deep breath, and think about what you're doing. This is guarantee verses unknown."

Penny answers, "I know, I just have faith. I can't explain it any better. It's something I just have to have faith that God can and will save Despair. It's going to be the same thing for me, which probably gives away what I'm going to choose, but I'll never know if I can be saved. I don't know if God can save a demon, even one who's been made mortal. I could be absolutely perfect down here and yeah, I understand my even thinking that I could be perfect is an ego thing, I'm working on it. I'm a work in progress. I don't know if I can be saved. I don't know if any demon can be saved, but I want to try and I don't want to torture anymore.

"I am not running away from you demons or the devil, who I know will be mad. I am more running toward a life where there is concern for others. Demons don't care about others, I do, or at least, I want to care more."

Penny turns and addresses the devil directly, "You were kicked out of Heaven because you refused to bow before God and do as God commanded. I am now choosing to not return to Hell because I no longer want to bow before you and I no longer want to do as you command. I understand by staying on Earth, I am giving up a lot of power and control. I understand there is no guarantee, that I can or will be saved. All I can tell you is, I can't go back. I care too much about mortals, including myself, to torture forever." Penny finishes her speech.

The devil not missing a beat addresses the class, "All right class real quick, Avarice is lead soul catcher. Envy is second lead soul catcher.

"I can't trust you, Envy. If any one knows the dangers of a rebellious upstart, it would be me. Unless any other of you want to stay on Earth, I suggest the rest of you follow me. Penny, You disappoint me."

Envy smiles and blows a kiss to Penny and says, "Can't wait to see you again."

With that the devil leads everyone down to room 13-18.j

———

Penny is left standing alone in the room. She know she would feel alone for a while, before she felt better.

The angel appears, puts her arm around her to comforts Penny and says, "It will take time, but you've made the right choice. You at least want to be a better person."

Chapter 24 Conclusion

The devil leads the class quickly through the doors of room 13-18. Once inside, the devil says, "Well that was an adventurous time on Earth, wasn't it? I assume all of you are anxious to get back to your existences in Hell.

"Avarice, I'll catch up with you later, today. Envy, same thing. No questions? Good, get out of my office."

Fallon watches all of this quietly. Upon the devil's command to get out of his office, Fallon ushers all the demons out the other door of the devil's office which, leads directly to Hell.

"I assume it was as we expected. I didn't see Penny, so I assume she decided to stay on Earth," Fallon says, cautiously.

The devil nods. "I, assume, we still have not heard regarding Despair?"

Fallon quietly answers, "No."

"Ok, so it's as we feared. I have lost two demons on this trip. I have not lost two demons in many, many years. One, I lose all the time. I never expect to get Despair back. All right, well, it is what it is. Anything else interesting going on?"

Fallon, wanting to give the devil some time and space, says, "Nothing too crazy" He shuffles some papers on the devil's desk and says, "Why don't I leave you and I will be back with some paperwork, later."

The devil answers, "Yes, that sounds fine." Fallon notices he sounded a little dejected.

———

Don't worry dear reader, I'm never down for long. Also don't worry about this story giving away too much of what's going on. You won't remember it, ten minutes after you put down this book, you'll suddenly get hungry for dinner. Maybe you'll think oh I better go check on the kids. You by no means are going to worry about your immortal soul.

Let's face it, there is no immortal soul. There is no God. You are only worried about this because you have just read a book about it. Come on, you're not even entirely sure God exists or maybe you are and that's ok.

Oh, next time you're out you better get to your car kind of quick that guy looks a little sketchy. I'll do whatever I have to do to distract you. You'll be slightly concerned about your fellow man. I mean you don't want to be stupid about it. That's good, that's good. Yeah, let's divide everyone up into an us and them. Remember, that helps me.

Let's face it people, it's not going to be long until you say to yourself: I'm a good person. I want good verifiable proof of God. Blind faith is a little bit much to be asking from people. I mean seriously with all the wars and the corruption and oh the scandals that have happened, it gets a person concerned.

Here's the thing, no matter how good God has created various religions or any collection of people, it's always people. There is nothing you can do. You can have a group of wonderful people, but here's the deal, they're mortal. They're going to be a mix of good and bad. If they weren't a mix of good and bad and they were truly all good, not a rotten bone in their body, well then they wouldn't need God. They wouldn't need Christ and then they'd be guilty of pride. Pride is a beautiful gateway sin. It's my favorite sin.

When the Catholic Church was found to have all these pedophiles and horrible people in there, I loved the finding of those people. Now, people use it as a reason, they do not belong to the church. It is understandable. It let me set up a beautiful US versus THEM. It drove a nice wedge. It also moved people slightly closer to questioning 'Is there really a God?' Come on now, is there really a God? You don't know. At best, you have faith. You don't have proof.

Heck, I'm here talking to you and people don't even question whether there's the devil. You know, they have the word atheist, which means I don't believe in God. Agnostic means lack of knowing God. There isn't an anti-Satanist or asantanist. There's no special word for 'I don't believe in the devil.' Technically, atheist would include God and the devil, but very few really use it that way. Even fewer understand it that way. This is to my benefit.

There is really no need for the word or oh, that's right I don't exist. Alright, let's leave it that way. I don't exist. There's no need for you to even think about this any further.

Let's leave it there, but you do have to admit, it is kind of fun. No one questions that I don't exist. Oh the things you can get away with when you don't exist.

I'm all bad. I'm ok with that. I could have served in Heaven. I chose to reign in Hell. I know who I am. I know what I believe. I'm already in Hell and I'm looking for company. So it kind of begs the question, are you going to come join me?

I'm not worried about losing Penny. I mean it sucks, don't get me wrong. She actually was a pretty good demon. There'll be another one along in a minute. They are easily replaceable.

I'm never down for long and you guys don't really let me go away.

I wish you'd let me work in the shadows. It's the end of the book. You probably have places to go, other things to think about. You just go ahead and forget about me. It's fine. It's like I don't even exist.

Suddenly, the loud booming voice of God, which makes the devil shudder, says:

"Fear not my readers. My will be done. I exist. If I did not, then how could he?

Chapter 25 Additional Chapter

Reader if you stop now, you have read the full book. You do not need to go further. It was a good solid happy ending, well an ending Penny still has work to do. God had the last word. If you continue on beyond this point, you're going to read a nice calm story with a disturbing ending. So if you're ok with being a little disconcerted, then by all means keep reading. If you would prefer to just have things end with God having the last word, then whatever you do - do not turn the page.

Gus, the dragon, walks down the cobblestone street. His large belly makes him have a kind of waddle but fortunately his tail prevents him from swaying too much. He arrives at Mrs. Scinter's house. She is at the stove. They exchange pleasantries and she says Hector is upstairs. Gus proceeds to go upstairs.

"Hi, Hector. Are you ready to hear the story of how the devil lost two demons?"

Hector looks at Gus wide eyed and says, "Did he lose them as in he misplaced them or did they get taken by the other side and yes, I'd love to hear the story."

Gus holds up a book and says, "Well worry not, I have the story right here. Believe it or not, he lost two demons within a few weeks. It just goes to show you that at times, anyone can be down."

Hector curled up next to Gus anxious to hear the story and just as Gus is about to begin, in walks Mrs. Scinter. Hector sees cookies and immediately moves. Mrs. Scinter has with her a tray and upon the tray is a plate of cookies and two glasses of tea. Well one's a regular cup of tea and the other is for Gus. He drinks his tea out of a very tall glass with a straw.

Hector looks at him quizzically, regarding the tall glass with the straw. Gus answers before being asked, "Big snout, little arms. It's best, I have my tea through a straw."

Hector smiles and asks Gus, "You're a nice dragon, why are you in Hell?"

Gus looks at Hector and says, "Mostly for job security. There's always a need for fire in Hell. There is not always a need for fire in Heaven. I mean sure the occasional pilot light goes out and that's when they need me.

"Also, when the unicorns have their barbecues. When they're having a barbecue, us dragons always get invited. Mostly to help light the grills. There is a problem with us going up for the unicorn barbecues, though. We love them don't get me wrong; but, when we go up there we end up sitting on clouds.

"I mean us dragons end up sitting on the clouds and we're kind of heavy. The clouds get these big black spots on them from where we're sitting on them. No sunlight can get past our bottoms. The humans look up from Earth and they think it's going to be a big rainstorm. It's a little embarrassing; but, still it's a nice barbecue. It's a bit of a break from the pace of Hell. Here you're always needed for lighting a fire or something." Gus, finishing his story, sipped his tea through the straw.

Gus quietly blows a small candle alive with a flame. Hector watches in awe and then in terror when Gus takes a large breath. Gus blows out the candelabra on the other side of the room, leaving only the small candle. Hector relaxes a bit.

Gus pulls him close and says, "Why are you so scared? You do know I can control how much fire comes out of me at any time."

Hector answers, "Nope, I didn't know you could do that. I just assumed you breathed fire all the time."

Gus answers, "If that were true, I'd have burned down my house a long time ago. My wife would have killed me. No, I can always decide how much fire comes out. Young dragons have problems controlling their fire; but, they figure it out within a year or so or they get really good at having a glass of water nearby. Now snuggle up and I will read you the book as promised about how the devil lost two demons in two weeks."

Hector curls up next to Gus, who puts an arm around him and opens his book. Gus begins reading:

"He walks in from the top doors of a lecture hall down to the podium. Everyone is turning, staring, they can't believe it's him. He's wearing a dark pinstriped suit. As he makes his way to the bottom of the stairs, he turns, and faces the class..."

See now you've read a nice story. Everything is fine and you can rest assured that - I don't exist.

Don't miss out!

Visit the website below and you can sign up to receive emails whenever Victoria W Thomson publishes a new book. There's no charge and no obligation.

https://books2read.com/r/B-A-VHIID-TMNOG

BOOKS 2 READ

Connecting independent readers to independent writers.

About the Author

Victoria W Thomson is a former attorney practicing mainly in bankruptcy law and wills, trusts, and estates. She left her law practice to be a stay-at-home mom. Her Multiple Sclerosis got worse and so she couldn't quilt anymore. Needing a new hobby, she decided to write a book after seeing a YouTube video advertising nanowrimo (national novel writing month) She did not write the book in a month. It took closer to 16 months. "He Who Does Not Exist" is her debut novel.